The Pickpocket Orphans

IRIS COLE

VIDORRA HOUSE

©Copyright 2022 Iris Cole

All Rights Reserved

License Notes

This Book is licensed for personal enjoyment only. It may not be resold. No part of this work may be reproduced in any form or by any electronic or mechanical means including information storage and retrieval systems, without written permission from the author.

Disclaimer

This story is a work of fiction, any resemblance to people is purely coincidence. All places, names, events, businesses, etc. are used in a fictional manner. All characters are from the imagination of the author.

Would you like a free book?

[CLAIM](https://dl.bookfunnel.com/kji81fn0dr)

[THE FOUNDLING BABY](https://dl.bookfunnel.com/kji81fn0dr)

[HERE](https://dl.bookfunnel.com/kji81fn0dr)

https://dl.bookfunnel.com/kji81fn0dr

Table of Contents

The Pickpocket Orphans .... *i*

Would you like a free book? .... *iv*

Prologue *1*

Chapter One *11*

Chapter Two *23*

Chapter Three *33*

Chapter Four *43*

Chapter Five *57*

Chapter Six *65*

Chapter Seven *77*

Chapter Eight *87*

Chapter Nine *101*

Chapter Ten *111*

Chapter Eleven *121*

Chapter Twelve *129*

Epilogue *141*

IRIS COLE

Prologue

Flurries of snow floated past the window, collecting in the runnels until peaks, like mountain ranges, formed upon the pane. Angel Gilmour, but eight years of age, huddled by the fire that raged in the grate of their apartments above the derelict remains of Royston & Sons Carpentry. Royston and his sons were naught but faded names upon the lintel of the former workshop now.

Unable to maintain the rents upon the building, they had sought out cheaper holdings. Meanwhile, none had come to take their place, making Angel and her father, George, ghosts within this derelict shell.

"It's fearsome cold tonight, Papa." Angel pulled a woollen blanket tighter about herself, in a vain attempt to keep out the biting draught. There was a reason these apartments had been so cheap.

Holes in the roof, cracks in the walls, an entire pane of glass missing where a stone had sailed through, and some floorboards that neither Angel nor her father dared to tread upon, lest they plummet through to the vacant workshop below. But it was home. A private realm for Angel and her father, where none could enter.

"That soup will be ready in no time." Her father entered, rubbing his wet hair with a threadbare rag. Angel had heard him break the ice that had settled on the basin, in his bedchamber, and knew his ablutions must have been icy.

Angel leaned forwards and used the edge of the blanket to lift the heavy lid of the pot that hung above the fire. "There are bubbles!"

George smiled fondly at his daughter. "What did I tell you? Almost ready."

Since her mother's death, some two years prior, it had only been the two of them.

Her father had never so much as contemplated remarriage, having loved his wife more than the Earth itself. Indeed, he had made a solemn promise, at his wife's graveside, that he would not so much as look at another woman.

Angel preferred it that way—just the two of them. They were each other's entire world, and she loved nothing more than to sit in this self-same spot and watch the door until her father returned from his daily business.

There, she would jump up and race towards him, throwing her arms about him and revelling in the joy of his return. And he would hold her back, twice as hard, to let her know that she had been equally as missed.

"Did you have a tiring day, Papa? Do you want to sit by the fire?" It was all she could offer him, for they had so little. And yet, her father never let their lack of means affect them.

There was always bread and butter and milk, and vegetables for broth, and even a scrap of meat here and there. Being so young, Angel never thought to ask where it came from.

George crossed the room and dipped low to kiss Angel upon the forehead. "You need it more than I do, my little chick. Warm yourself. I'll be well enough once I've some soup in my belly."

Angel glowed with happiness and checked the pot again. She was just about to declare it ready for consumption, when a loud bang at the door splintered through their calm serenity. She jolted in fright, a shiver running through her, though she did not believe it could be from the cold. No, she was too near to the fire for that.

"Mr. George Gilmour; are you in there?" a gruff, deep voice barked behind the security of the front door. Three black iron bolts held it closed from the inside, though the wood shuddered as another bang hammered upon it.

Angel peered up at her father in fright. "Who is"

She did not get to finish as her father hurried to his knees and clamped his hand over her mouth. His eyes lifted wide, like those of a spooked horse preparing to bolt. "Say nothing," he whispered. "Go to the trunk in your bedchamber and hide there until I tell you it is safe to come out. Do you understand? Don't make a single sound while you're in there. Stay quiet as a mouse, little chick. Quiet as a mouse."

Terror seized her heart in a vice. "But, Papa..." The sound came out muffled, with his fingers still tight across her mouth.

"There is no time, little chick. Go to the trunk. Hide there. Go now," he urged, a sudden sadness appearing in his eyes. A sadness she could not have understood, then.

"George Gilmour!" a different voice, sharper than before, bellowed. "Open up! We know you're in there—you were seen entering not twenty minutes ago!"

George pulled Angel into his arms and whispered in her ear. "I love you, my sweet, sweet girl. You have to hide now, but it won't be for long. I need to speak with these men, and then we can eat our soup and I'll read you a story before you go to sleep. Any story you like. I'll make one up for you."

Angel nodded slowly and George released his grip on her mouth. "I love you too, Papa. Promise you won't leave me for long? It's dusty in that trunk, and there are spiders."

"I promise," he replied and, God bless her, she believed him.

On shaky legs, she let her father help her to her feet. All the while, the explosions of fists upon the door continued, the wood shuddering more violently with every impact.

George pushed her towards her bedchamber and, though she hesitated for a moment upon the threshold, she did as he had asked. But not without casting him one last, frightened look. He smiled back and pressed his fingers to his lips, blowing her a kiss for courage. Drawing upon it, she turned and disappeared into the darkness.

In the gloom of her room, she scurried across the creaky floor, much like the mouse he had told her to be, and carefully lifted the heavy lid of the old trunk that once held all of their belongings.

She did not need a light to see by; she would have known every inch of this bedchamber with her eyes closed. Still, she paused once more, listening out as the bangs upon the front door grew more insistent.

Don't leave me too long, Papa. I don't much like the dark. With a deep breath, she clambered into the trunk and closed the lid as softly as possible. It closed with a dull thud, plunging her into complete shadow.

Clawing at the musty wood with her nails, she manoeuvred herself until her eye was pressed up against the keyhole. From there, she could see the faint glow of the parlour, the flames making the light dance against the distant doorframe.

"George Gilmour!" the first voice called again, followed by a crack so loud she thought a thunderstorm had rolled into the apartments. Something had splintered. Something had broken. Her terrified mind thought of the front door and wondered if those gruff men had shattered one of the locks.

Another deafening crack came soon after, prompting Angel to tuck her knees to her chin, making herself as small as possible. Still, she kept one eye on the keyhole.

A shadow darted across the open doorway beyond. Her father. She heard a ruckus from the room beside hers, which served as her father's bedchamber. Pots crashing and metal clanking to the ground, and the tell-tale smash of a window being broken.

"Gilmour!" the second voice howled. A third lightning crack pounded in Angel's ears, though it may have been the blood rushing by.

All of a sudden, two strangers raced across the open doorway, dressed in the uniforms of the London constabulary.

Their silver adornments glinted as they rushed by. More strange sounds ensued, as if they were intent upon destroying her father's bedchamber entirely.

I must help him! Her young mind was frantic with worry, but she could not move a muscle.

Her father had urged her to stay here until the trouble had passed, and she was more afraid of making him cross than what might happen to her if she emerged.

A moment later, the two strangers hauled her father back into the parlour. She heard the scrape of handcuffs as the first stranger—a broad, grizzled individual—shoved her father to his knees.

"George Gilmour, you are being arrested on the charge of grand theft," the man announced, as he clapped her father's wrists in those vile cuffs and turned the key in the lock.

George twisted his head up to glare at the constable. "I haven't stolen anything! I'm innocent of this! Unhand me, and take off these chains.

I don't know who's been telling you these lies, but I'm not the man you're looking for!"

Angel trembled inside the trunk, not understanding what was going on.

The second constable—a thinner man with equally thin hair—snorted. "Nice try, Gilmour. There are witnesses who saw what you did. Powerful witnesses, who've got proof. You shouldn't have stolen from rich folks, Gilmour. It always ends like this."

Stolen? Papa? No... Papa would never steal!

Angel pulled her blanket tighter around herself. This was all a huge misunderstanding. It had to be. Her father was a good man. He would never take anything that did not belong to him.

She watched and waited, but her father said nothing. All his protestations of innocence had died upon his lips.

Tell them, Papa! Tell them you didn't do what they think you did! She tried to urge the message into his mind, but it did no good. He knelt there, silent as a grave, until the constables hauled him to his feet and dragged him away. Angel pressed her eye closer to the keyhole, not knowing what to do.

An hour passed. Maybe more. Maybe less. Time had lost all meaning in the dusty darkness of the trunk. Finally, she found the courage to lift the lid and climb out. Sucking in shallow breaths, she edged towards the still-open doorway and poked her head around the frame. The parlour lay empty, a bitter wind screaming in through the gaping front door.

She sprinted for it, and slammed it shut, but the bolts were broken. Staggering away from the door, she retreated to her usual spot by the fire and sat there, not caring that the soup bot was boiling over. Here, she was determined to wait until her father came back, just as he had promised.

It would be like the daytime, when he went away to work. He would come back. He would step through that door, and she would throw her arms about him again and warm him with soup and blankets, and an insistence that he take her spot by the fire.

Only, this time... he did not come back.

Chapter One

Ten Years Later

Angel ducked under the low lintel of the dilapidated galley that served as her kitchen, her plain lavender dress always smelling faintly of bacon and woodsmoke. The beams of the old ship creaked and the scent of the Thames, foetid and earthy, rose up through the mouldering wood.

She did not know how her employer and saviour, Donald McIntyre, had found this wreckage, or how he had come to purchase it, but it had been her home for the last ten years. Nestled along the banks of the river, it looked abandoned to the unknowing eye. However, within, it brimmed with youthful life.

Ten pairs of eyes stared back at her as she produced a long, woollen coat and hung it from the back of the nearest door, making sure all of the bells were in place—alerts, which would jangle if one of her acolytes failed to steal what resided in the coat pockets.

"Solomon, if you'd like to go first?" Angel prompted, spotting her favourite at the back of the group. She didn't like to have favourites, not really, but she could not help but adore Solomon's big dark eyes and feline face, which reminded her so much of a lost kitten in need of love and care.

Solomon puffed out a sigh. "Do I 'ave to?"

"No, you don't have to, but I've asked you to." Angel smiled, knowing he would do it. For he was fond of her, too. She had been the one to bring him into McIntyre's gang, after finding him alone, and frozen, and half-dead upon a street corner the winter just gone.

An orphan, or as good as, like the rest of these children. She'd been the same when Donald had found her, wandering the streets, barefoot in the snow, after her father had been taken away.

She owed him her life. She had waited for two days in their empty apartments, praying for her father's return, as he had promised. When he had not appeared, she had gone in search of him, starved and weary to the point of exhaustion. She had walked miles to this very riverbank, unable to feel the cold due to the numbness in her heart.

That was where Donald had found her, and taken her under his wing, transforming her from helpless little girl into independent, skilled pickpocket.

Now, at eighteen years of age, she held the record for spending the most time in this role without a single arrest.

Ten years, to be precise. With her deft hands and light fingers, she could lift just about anything from any pocket. And now, she gifted her expertise to the children who came on-board the Salty Serpent, seeking the same purpose and companionship that she had, once upon a time.

Solomon pushed through the raggedy bunch of children and put his hands behind his back, assessing the coat. Angel watched him with a smile, as he crossed back and forth, before darting forward and sliding his hand into the pocket. He almost had the wallet loose, when the bell jangled.

"Too rash, Solomon," Angel chided softly. The nine other children chuckled to themselves, gaining a stern look from their teacher. "I wouldn't be so quick to judge, if I were you. You're all to take a turn at trying to get what's in those pockets. Line up, all of you. If the bell rings, go to the back of the line and try again, until the bell doesn't ring."

"Can't we just try it on the streets?" another boy, by the name of Davis, complained.

"Do you know what happens instead of a bell jangling, when you're out on the streets, Davis?" Angel folded her arms across her chest.

"You get caught!" Sally, one of the little girls, shouted.

Angel nodded. "Precisely. You get caught, then you get locked up, and we don't have the money to bail you out. So, practise, practise, practise, until that bell don't ring."

Nervous chatter filled the room, as the children obeyed. Angel watched, and offered advice to each child, as they made their first attempts.

She glanced over to the far side of the room, now and again, to find some of the old hands spectating. These were the older children, who'd been lucky enough to avoid being arrested, or had already served their time and had been released.

Angel hated to see the hardness in their young faces, and the vacant stare of their eyes.

Few made it out of this life unaltered, and it broke her heart every time. Truly, she did not know how she had managed to survive this underworld without it stealing away her very soul. But she had.

"You know it won't do 'em no good." Harry, one of the older children, muttered from the back of the room. "I never let that bell ring, and I've been in the clink twice."

"You get overexcited," Angel replied, hoping it didn't unnerve the younger children. "That is why you were caught."

Harry shrugged. "Who's to say it won't be the same for these? They'd be better off swimming to one of them prison ships on the horizon and skipping the bit in-between."

The younger children stared at Angel with frightened eyes.

"You're still here, aren't you?" she said curtly, flashing Harry a warning look.

"Aye, by the skin of me teeth." Harry grinned, and the younger children seemed satisfied that he was only joking.

All in all, this was not such a bad life, considering the alternative. Here, they had food, and shelter, and a sense of purpose.

For Angel, her purpose had altered somewhat— now, it was her primary joy and focus, to take care of these children and make sure as few as possible ended up in the hands of the London Constabulary.

She may not have remembered her own mother, but she had become one to a multitude of children, who looked up to her, and relied upon her for safety and comfort.

Still, as their sometime mother, it wounded her when, inevitably, they were captured in the act of their underhanded work.

That was why she showed such diligence in their pickpocketing education, even though instinct and nerves played a much larger role when it came to them actually heading into the streets.

Some of the children could be retrieved when they found themselves in the hands of the law, but some were never heard from again.

It broke Angel's heart when they did not come back, but that perpetual loss only made her all the more determined to show them some shred of kindness whilst they were under her care.

"I did it!" Solomon whirled around on his third attempt, with the wallet clutched in his hand. Sure enough, the bells upon the overcoat remained undisturbed.

Angel smiled. "Very good, Solomon, though I wouldn't suggest you show your victory until you're far away from whomever you stole from." She flashed him a reassuring wink, and the other children laughed warmly.

"Of course not." Solomon beamed proudly. Angel was careful not to show any sorrow upon her face, for now that he had managed the task of taking the wallet, Donald would expect him to try it in the real world beyond this peculiar haven. She knew it had to happen.

For her part, she had still not learned that it was imprudent to have favourites. It simply made her position aboard this stationary husk of a ship that much harder.

At that moment, the sound of heavy footsteps permeated the room, thudding along the old floorboards. Angel knew the sound, her head turning as Donald McIntyre himself appeared under the low lintel of the doorway.

A thick-set man in his early forties, with a surprisingly full head of reddish-bronzed hair, faintly flecked with grey, Donald's keen blue eyes surveyed the scene before him. The ginger of his whiskers twitched as a smile pulled at his lips.

"I hope you're not spoiling them, Angel?" he said, in his deep, gravelly voice, which still held the mildest twang of his Scottish origins.

"Not at all," she replied. "A last-minute instruction before they go out."

He nodded, fixing his gaze upon her. "Very well, then it's due time they were off to their duties, eh? There's work te be done and coin te be made! And I'll give a silk handkerchief te the first one of ye that can bring me back a gold pocket watch."

The children gasped and their eyes glinted with excitement, but Angel's heart sank. She wished he would not set them such challenges, for it inspired the children to be rash.

And to make mistakes that they would not otherwise make. Nevertheless, she knew better than to question Donald in front of his multitude of wards.

She clapped her hands together to draw back their attention. "Mr. McIntyre's right—you ought to be on your way. To those who are new to this, you stay with those who know what they're doing. Let them lead and learn what you can. And, remember our motto?"

"Stay alert and think quick, and don't end up in the nick!" they chorused.

"Exactly," Angel said quietly. "Now, be on your way. I expect to see every single one of you back here by evening."

She ushered them toward the main entrance of the ship and watched as they slunk out in pairs and trios, settling into natural teams. She stood there until the last of them had departed, wishing she could offer more to each of them than this life. For, in her heart of hearts, she knew there would always be an evening when they did not all come back.

"You care too much." Donald appeared at her side, though Angel did not turn to look at him.

Instead, she shook her head. "No, I care as much as I ought to. These children have no-one and nothing, so I may as well be the one to give them something in this world that's not harsh or cruel or cold. There'll be enough of that when they get older."

If they get older... Sickness was as much a threat to the children as capture.

"If I've said it once, I'll say it again—you were named just right when you came into this world." Donald chuckled. "Fortune made us cross paths that day, when you were only a wee one yourself. I believe it with my whole heart. I'd never have managed any of this—not so smoothly, at least—without ye."

Angel sighed. "Don't, Donald."

"Ah, but I've got te, Angel. I'm not one to give up, and I'll keep asking until the day comes where ye say yes." He put his hand upon her shoulder and squeezed it gently. "Will ye no marry me, Angel Gilmour? Will ye no make me the happiest man in England?"

At last, she turned and met his gaze. "Not today, Donald."

Each day, they shared the same exchange. He asked, and she refused. A game they played, though Angel worried that Donald truly believed that, one of these days, he would gain a different reply. She could not deny that, with each instance, it left her feeling uncomfortable, but she had grown accustomed to this repartee between them.

And he would never dare to force my hand... would he? The fearful uncertainty lingered as Donald mustered another low chuckle, and walked away from her, disappearing into the belly of the ship to organise the horde of treasure that had been collected yesterday. A veritable dragon, coveting his ill-gotten gains.

Chapter Two

Ominous clouds of swollen, dark grey gathered overhead as Angel took to the streets in search of her wayward children.

It had been several days since she had first sent Solomon out to perform his expected duties, and though he had returned each evening, having been under the care and protection of the older children, the idea of waiting within the sometimes suffocating confines of the old ship had been too much for her that morning.

As such, she found herself upon the streets close to the impressive architecture of St. Paul's Cathedral, where the wealthy mingled with the unfortunates in the chilly late morning.

She drew her woollen shawl tighter about herself, in a vain attempt to deter the cold from penetrating. In retaliation, it nipped all the harder at her cheeks.

"Morning, Angel!" one of the tinkers, pushing along his cart of wares, tipped his cap to her as she passed by.

"Morning, Dickinson," she answered in kind, with a nod of her head. This was one of her unruly brood's preferred spots for pickpocketing, and there were not many of London's underbelly who did not recognise her.

There was an unspoken rule that, so long as the children did not interfere with others of their social standing, they did not interfere in their affairs either. Indeed, over her ten years under Donald's watch, she had come to call many of them acquaintances and even friends.

"Can I interest you in some gloves? Or, perhaps, a new poker for your fire?" Dickinson gestured to his cart, but Angel shook her head.

"No, thank you. I've not got the coin."

He smiled. "Right you are, Angel. Don't you go getting yourself in trouble, you hear?"

"I won't." She managed a quiet laugh. "Same goes for you."

She pressed on along the streets, spying small clusters of the children as they went about their daily toil.

Wherever possible, she stayed close to them, without infringing upon their space. That way, if anything went awry, she would be able to run interference—another skill she had learned in her years of doing this.

There were not many situations she could not talk her way out of. As she wandered, maintaining an air of casual nonchalance, she proceeded to do some pickpocketing of her own.

It always helped to have some extra pieces, to cover any deficits the children might have faced.

Donald did not expect her to do the dirty work any longer, but she did not mind, if it helped the children. And she did have such supremely deft hands.

Sauntering beside two tall, fine gentlemen in expensive tailoring, she walked slightly ahead of them and paused to look at some of the flowers being sold by the side of the road by a small, dirt-streaked girl and her haggard mother.

Using her instincts, she waited until the gentlemen were almost upon her before stepping back into their path.

She bumped directly into the nearest fellow. As expected, his hands shot out to steady her as she made a charade of stumbling and almost falling.

"Goodness! My apologies, sir—I didn't see you there!" She acted flustered as his attention focused upon her pretty features.

He did not know that, if he were to look into his right-hand pocket, he would find his wallet missing.

Quick as a flash, whilst his hands had been upon her back, she had slid her hand into the pocket and taken the item, before tucking it under the edge of her shawl.

"That is quite all right, Miss. Although, you ought to be more careful where you tread," he warned, not unkindly.

"I will, sir. Thank you for catching me." She fluttered her eyelashes and offered him her most endearing smile. His expression softened, and he finally removed his hands from her.

"I am only glad that I could be of service." He tipped his hat to her, before carrying on his way with his acquaintance. It was another fact of life that she had learned—if one was pretty enough, one could fox just about anyone.

Once they were gone, Angel turned and took out a coin, before handing it to the wretched pair of flower sellers.

"You want a rose for that?" the mother asked, with a smirk. "They should put up a statue for ye, Angel, with skills like yours. I bet that fella will get a nasty surprise when he checks his pockets."

Angel laughed, though it echoed false. Despite her expertise in the field of theft, she never felt good about stealing.

The way she viewed it, it was a means to an end, and she was simply doing whatever she could to survive. "You keep your flowers for other customers. All I want for that coin is your continued silence." She winked, knowing she could rely on these people.

"Aye, you know I'll not say aught," the woman assured her.

"Thank you, Lucy."

With a nod, Angel continued along the street, slipping the pilfered wallet discreetly into the pockets that she had sewn into her dress for just such a purpose.

After an hour or so of watching the children from afar, and taking a few more items from the wealthy elite who happened to be unfortunate enough to cross her path, she paused upon the corner of a road and wondered if she ought to buy something to eat from the nearby bakery.

It was during this moment of quiet contemplation that her eyes settled on the street opposite.

A figure stood there, beside the black sentinel of a lamppost, watching her. Her forehead furrowed as she squinted for a better view, the figure flashing in between the carousel of carriages that thundered by.

Her heart lurched.

No... it can't be... And yet, she would have known that face anywhere.

It was seared into her memory, as though God Himself had branded it upon her mind. He looked older and thinner, with sunken cheeks and a drawn, pallid complexion, with his dark hair swept in a neatened style.

But it was him. It could not be anyone else. Yes, he looked ten years older than the last time she had seen him, being dragged away by constables from their home.

"Papa!" she blurted out instinctively.

The figure's eyes widened; his expression sad. But he did not call back to her.

The carriages continued to rattle past at alarming speed, giving her glimpses of the man she knew to be her father.

Panic rose through her, her legs itching to run across the road to him. However, such actions would have been unwise. She had witnessed many a tragic injury, or worse, when people had tried to cross such roads in a hurry. And so, she hovered desperately for a moment, until a safe gap appeared in the equine traffic.

At last, such a gap appeared. She put out a foot to cross the road, only to halt abruptly. Her father no longer stood on the opposite street.

Her eyes darted frantically from left to right, to try and spot him in the crowds that walked there, but she could not see him anywhere.

He had gone. And, in truth, she was no longer certain he had ever been there in the first place.

I saw him. I know I saw him. He was there... he was really there. During her first year without him, she had done all she could to try and find him, but had been met with the stony silence of the London Constabulary, who thought her a pest.

Had she been older, and more beautiful, as she was now, perhaps she might have had more success. However, back then, nobody had cared to listen to a bereft child. And why would they, when London's streets were filled with orphans?

She was about to cross, regardless, when a sharp, startled cry splintered the air. It was followed, a second later, by the frightened whinny of a horse, and the disgruntled shout of another individual. Her head whipped around. A short distance away, a carriage had come to a standstill.

Around it, a crowd had already begun to gather. Fearing that something might have happened to one of the children, she raced towards the scene.

"What's happened?" she gasped, drawing close.

"A boy's been hit," one of the macabre observers replied.

"A boy?" Her heart hammered in her chest as she pushed her way forwards. Reaching the front line of spectators, she had to reach out to one of them to steady herself, for her knees almost buckled beneath her as she looked upon the tragedy.

A painfully small figure lay in the dirt, blood pooling from a brutal injury to the head, where half a face had once been—so brutal and upsetting that she had to force herself to keep looking. The liquid sank into the ground, turning it a muddied scarlet.

Oh, my poor, poor, sweet Solomon... She staggered forwards and fell to her knees beside him, tentatively brushing the wayward strands of hair out of his mangled face. Tears trickled down her cheeks before she could stop them, and a bestial howl screamed from the back of her throat, frightening the spectators into shamefacedness.

But she did not care for them. She could think only of Solomon, and the life that had been stolen from him.

"I'm sorry, Solomon. I'm so very sorry." She bent forwards and pressed her forehead to his chest, as she took his still-warm hand in hers. Lifting her head slightly, she saw that his kind eyes stared upwards vacantly, the life having already left him.

This was one situation that she could not talk her way out of. No, this she could not fix.

Chapter Three

"Angel?" Two of the other children, who had been teamed with Solomon, approached anxiously. A young girl by the name of Elise, and one of the older boys, Leon. Elise had tears running down her rosy cheeks and could not look at the broken form of Solomon. Even Leon did not seem to be able to look.

Angel knew why. Solomon had been put into Leon's care, and the older boy had failed him. Not that Angel would ever blame Leon for this tragedy — he was just a child himself.

"Return to the Serpent." Angel fought to control her overwhelming grief. "Round up the others and get them to go back, too. If Mr. McIntyre asks why, you tell him I gave the order and will explain it all to him later. And take these."

Discreetly, she palmed the wallets and trinkets she had stolen into Elise's skirts, in the hopes it would mollify Donald when he discovered that his entire contingent of pickpockets had returned early.

"Shouldn't we stay with you?" Leon asked sheepishly.

Angel shook her head. "No. Go back, before the constables arrive. They'll want to know what happened here, and I don't want them using it as an excuse to search you all."

In a gesture of kindness, Leon took Elise by the hand and led her away. And not a moment too soon. With her eyes blurred from her own tears, Angel looked up to find a constable walking in her direction.

The uniform was unmistakable. He was younger than most, however, with a mass of dark curls beneath his hat, and concerned green eyes that did not leave her face. S

he might have thought him handsome, with his youthful, masculine features and smattering of freckles, had she not despised any man who wore that uniform.

Your ilk took my father away, and I'll never forgive that. Her mind drifted back to the figure on the opposite side of the road.

As the time passed, she grew more and more uncertain of whether she had actually seen him, or whether it had been her idle mind playing cruel tricks upon her.

Either way, it had reminded her of her contempt for constables, and the supposed justice system that had taken her father from her.

"Miss?" The constable crouched in front of her, though Solomon's body lay between them. She hated that he dared to come so close to the young boy whom she adored as though he were her own brother, or son.

Yet, she knew she had to maintain an air of civility. Rudeness and derision would get her nowhere.

"Yes," she replied stiffly.

"My name is Constable Milton—Jimmy Milton. Can you tell me what occurred here?" He spoke softly, his tone calm and oddly melodic.

Annoyance spiked in her chest. "A boy is dead, Constable."

"I can see that, and I can see that it has affected you greatly. Was he family to you? Did you see what happened to him?"

"He was as good as family to me. As for what happened—a carriage ran him down. I didn't see the incident, but it's not hard to figure out." She dug her fingernails into her palms, realising that her attempts at civility were falling far short.

He nodded, evidently unperturbed by her cold demeanour. "Then, I am sorry for your loss, Miss. My partner has already gone for the mortuary cart. It will not be long until it arrives. I can disperse this crowd for you, if you'd prefer? I've never understood why folks seem intent on getting a glimpse of a dead body, especially a child."

His words took her aback. "Why should you be sorry? To you, it's just another orphan off the street and out of trouble."

"That isn't true, Miss. It's a terrible thing, to witness the death of any child, no matter who they may be, or where they've come from."

His eyes refused to leave hers, and she felt irritated that his soft voice should be making her feel soothed in her grief.

As such, she unleashed a torrent of emotion in his direction, her broken heart turning her words cold and bitter.

"You expect me to believe that? Why are you even talking to me? Are you trying to relieve your conscience, or something? I don't want your questions, Constable. How can I even think, when a little boy is dead between us—a little boy who can expect nothing but a pauper's grave; his name forgotten within the year by everyone but me," she ranted, her cheeks hot and fierce with misery.

Jimmy sat back on his haunches, visibly chastened. "I didn't mean to cause you further upset, Miss. I'll leave you be, so you can grieve in peace." He paused. "But may I know your name, so I'll know who's responsible for this child?"

"My name is Angel, though I notice you haven't bothered to ask for the child's name," she spat. "Does he not matter to you? I thought he did, since that's what you claimed not a moment ago."

"I'm sorry again, Miss. That was foolish of me. What is the child's name?" He finally looked away, embarrassed.

Her expression hardened. "His name was Solomon Fincher. And I hope that, with every year that passes, you don't forget his name like everyone else will."

"I won't," he replied, seemingly earnest. "I won't forget either of you."

Angel snorted. "I don't believe a word."

"Nevertheless, it's the truth." He stood up slowly and bent his head. "I'll leave you now. I shouldn't have bothered you, when you're clearly suffering. However, if there's anything you need, you've only to ask."

Angel said nothing and sullenly returned to her quiet vigil at Solomon's side, whilst Jimmy walked away and went to speak with the driver of the carriage that had caused Solomon's death.

She could not hear what was being said, nor did she want to. She knew how this society worked. The driver would evade any retribution for his actions, and it would be named an unfortunate accident, caused by the wayward behaviour of a wretched child who ran into the road, when he ought to have shown more care.

So, it came as quite the surprise, when Jimmy returned ten minutes later.

"I thought you said you would leave me be?" she said frostily.

He nodded. "I did, but there's something I thought you should know. I spoke with the driver of the carriage that killed this boy, and he, in turn, spoke with the passenger—a wealthy gentleman who is eager to be on his way. I said I would allow him to leave in another carriage and would come to speak with him later about what had happened, if he agreed to pay compensation for the boy." He produced a note—more money than Angel had ever seen, in one place, in a long while. "With this, I will make sure that Solomon has a stone to mark his grave, in a real cemetery, where you can visit him as you please."

Angel blinked in surprise. "Why?" She had never known a constable do anything to help someone like her, or someone like Solomon.

"Because it pains me, to see a young woman so injured. And it pains me all the more, when high society escape all manner of justice, simply because they're rich."

He mustered a small, sad smile. "We can't change the way things are, Miss, but we can get what we can and make it work for our benefit. I can tell you where he's to be buried, once I've made arrangements, if you'd like?"

Her heart broke all over again. "I... would like that." The words stuck somewhat in her throat, for she was unused to speaking kindly to a man like him. And yet, how could she continue in her cold tone, when he was offering such a gift?

"Where can I find you?" He peered deeper into her eyes, making her feel most peculiar.

Her chest clenched suddenly, as she realised what he had asked. She could not very well give him the address of the Salty Serpent, considering what she did there, and considering the safety of the other children in her care.

"I... will find you, Constable," she answered, after a pause. "Once I have seen Solomon to the mortuary, I will find you."

He nodded. "As you wish, Miss."

Angel did not yet know how she would muster the courage to set foot in a constabulary, after all these uniformed cretins had done to destroy her life.

And yet, all she had to do was look down at the ruined face of dear, sweet Solomon, and she knew she would go wherever she had to, in order to ensure that he had a final resting place that she could go to, if only to say that she was sorry for the short life he had endured.

Yes, for Solomon's sake, she would tread into Hell itself.

Chapter Four

George Gilmour had spent nine years enduring the pain and torment of hard labour, all the while contemplating what he would do upon the instance of his release.

There had not been a single day where he had not thought of his daughter, whom he had been forced to abandon on that fateful night, when the constables had taken him away. Indeed, he firmly believed that the sole reason he had survived his sentence was because of his constant thoughts of her.

He had refused to die without seeing her again. It was as simple as that.

And yet... he had been released almost a year ago, having not so much as caught a glimpse of the daughter he adored with his whole heart.

Although, it was not for lack of trying. He had sought her out through every possible avenue, to no avail.

There had been no trace of her amongst his old acquaintances, for they had not seen her since she was a child, and he had no fresh leads to follow.

But she is not a child anymore. He stood in the shadows of an alleyway, his back pressed to the grimy wall, pausing to catch his breath.

He had all but given up hope of ever seeing Angel again, until he had happened to spot her on the opposite street, not an hour ago. A true miracle of fate that he had not expected.

So, why did I run? Why am I hiding, when I ought to be out there, speaking with her? He shook his head crossly, furious with himself.

After all, he was a far better man than he had been when he had been arrested.

Proving his skill as a carpenter, using the expertise he had attained in his nine years of prison.

Now he was employed in a shipyard, where he had made a tidy sum for himself. In addition, he now had clean apartments where his rents were always paid on time, and he never went hungry.

I hid out of guilt, he realised. He regretted leaving her in the manner he had, on that snowy night.

During his sentence, he had often wondered how long she had stayed there, in the apartment, waiting for him to return as he had promised to.

And, every time he thought of it, it stung like a barb. He had never intended to disappoint her, or leave her alone in this world, and it agonised him to know that his foolish actions had caused him to do just that.

But she is alive, and she saw me. And I can't let her down again. He rallied, his heart swelling with renewed determination.

Yes, he may have been afraid of a frosty reception, and he may have been fearful that too many years had gone by for their relationship to be salvaged, but he had to try, at the very least. *I will find her again, and, this time, I will swallow my fears. I won't run and I won't hide. She deserves more from me, after what I did.*

The only trouble was, he did not know where to begin with finding her again.

Worried that he may have lost the chance for good, he slipped back out of the alleyway and returned to the street where he had spied her. This time, he crossed over to the other side and spent another half an hour searching for Angel amongst the crowds. But she had gone, and none could tell him where she had vanished to.

"Do you mean Angel?" A flower seller squinted up at him through rheumy eyes, as he stopped to ask if the woman had seen his daughter. He had given a brief description of her, in the hopes it might prompt a memory.

George's heart leapt. "Yes, Angel. Have you seen her?"

The flower-seller shrugged. "She were here about an hour ago, or so. A boy died—got knocked down by a carriage. I think she went with the mortuary cart. Can't be sure, though."

"Do you know where she lives?" George pressed.

"Not a clue. She's like a ghost, that one—appears and disappears, just like that."

The flower-seller flashed a partially toothed grin. "Or maybe she's more like her namesake, eh? All I know is, I see her most often when I'm selling me wares in the docks, but you've a fair stretch of 'em if you're wanting to look for her there."

"Is there anyone else who might be able to help me find her?" George felt his optimism deflating by the second.

The flower-seller paused in thought. "Aye, she were speaking with some constable or other. Milton, I think his name were. He said he'd help her out with the boy's grave. I shouldn't have been listening in, but it's hard not to, sometimes."

"Who was this boy?" George's eyes widened, as every possibility thrummed through his mind. "Was he her son?"

"Lord, no!" The flower-seller chuckled. "He were just some boy, but she's got a soft spot for the orphans of this here city. Anyway, if you're wanting to find her, you could go speak to that constable. Or, you could just wait around here in the hopes she'll reappear. She comes by sometimes, but I couldn't tell you when she'll next be around."

"I don't have time for that," he replied quietly. "Thank you for your help."

"Ah, think nought of it." The flower-seller waved her hand at him.

Knowing she deserved compensation for her information, he delved into his pocket and took out two coins, before handing them to her. "Here."

"You're too kind, sir." She bit the coin to check it was legitimate, but he did not judge her for it. Once upon a time, he would have done the same thing.

With that, he turned away and headed directly for Bow Street, where he hoped he might be able to discover this Milton character. If he could not, he knew he would have to resort to the flower-seller's other suggestion—that he wait and he wait and he wait until Angel happened to appear again.

But he had meant what he said. He truly did not know if he had the time for that, not because he lacked the patience, but because he lacked the health.

After taking a hackney carriage to Bow Street, regardless of the expense, he alighted there.

Waiting a moment, he gathered his courage and strode directly into the building that had become famous for its constables. Men in uniform bustled hither and thither, paying him little heed.

Truly, it felt rather uncomfortable for him to find himself in such an establishment, considering his history with the law. And yet, determination to find his daughter spurred him on to approach the reception, where a bored-looking fellow languished behind a desk, drumming his fingertips upon the varnished surface.

"Excuse me, do you know if I might be able to find a Constable Milton here?" George asked, without preamble.

The fellow looked up with heavily hooded eyes. "You mean Jimmy Milton?"

"Perhaps. Was he the constable on duty around St. Paul's earlier today?"

The fellow puffed out a breath. "Ah, you must be here about the carriage incident? The one that killed one of them orphans?"

"Uh... yes. I am here to speak with Constable Milton about it," George replied, though it was only half the truth.

"Stay here, and I'll get him for you. He only just came back from the mortuary." The fellow got up and disappeared through a door behind him, leaving George to scour the room for a place to sit. The building smelled of tobacco smoke and fear, with a tinge of sweat and destitution.

It made for a heady aroma, that turned George's stomach. He did not want to be here, and he certainly did not want to speak with a constable, but necessity called for it.

He crossed the main room to a narrow bench to one side, and was about to sit, when the glib fellow returned with another man in tow.

Without bothering to call George back over, the fellow from the desk muttered something to the other man and gestured casually in George's direction, before returning to his seat. The epitome of laziness.

Nevertheless, the other fellow followed the gesture and headed for George.

"Constable Faulks said you wanted to speak with me?" he said, putting out his hand. "I'm Constable Jimmy Milton."

George cleared his throat and shook the proffered hand. "I'm George Gilmour. I was wondering if I could talk to you for a minute, about someone you might've seen today."

He paused uncertainly and forced himself to continue. In truth, he needed help. Any help. "You see, I'm looking for my daughter—she and I were separated ten years ago, and I've been searching for her ever since, without success."

He paused again, aware they were in a rather public place. "I've got reason to believe you might've met her today, and I was hoping I might be able to get your help, to track her down."

Jimmy's eyes flew wide in surprise. "Do you mean Angel?"

It seems she is quite well known for someone who's been impossible to locate. He supposed there was a bitter sense of irony to that.

He nodded. "Yes, that's my daughter. Does this mean you did meet her today?"

"Briefly," Jimmy confirmed. "But I've got business with her. I'm just waiting for her to come here, so that I can proceed with it."

"Business?" George arched an eyebrow. He did not like the sound of that.

"Oh, it's nothing underhand, I assure you," Jimmy hastened to explain. "You see, I arranged for a gravestone for the boy who died today—he seemed to be a ward of hers, or something like that. I think she was worried he'd end up in a pauper's grave, so I said I'd sort out an alternative for the poor child, so she'd have a place to visit him."

"Why would you do that?" George blurted out, prompting the constable to laugh wryly.

"People keep asking me that." He gave a slight shrug. "I don't like to see people sad, and I don't like to see children dead in the street, destined for an unmarked grave where they'll not be remembered by anyone. If that makes me odd, then I guess I'm odd."

George nodded uncertainly, wondering if he could trust this strange individual. "Would you be willing to help me find Angel, then, if you already have your own reason to speak with her?" He decided that he would have to have faith in this man, if he hoped to locate Angel whilst he still had breath in his lungs.

"I could pass a message to her when she comes here, if you've the time to wait?" Jimmy suggested. It did make the greatest sense, yet it was not enough to satisfy George.

"I'm afraid it must be quicker than that. I heard she can often be seen along the docks, though I don't know that I can search them all on my own." *I do not even know if I can search a single one on my own.* He remained silent about the latter thought, for the sake of his own dignity.

Jimmy smiled. "Fear not. If that's where she's been seen, then that's where we'll find her. Although, I'll be sure to let you know if she visits here first, to save some trouble. Either way, you can count on me, Mr. Gilmour."

"I've got to say it again, and I know this sounds impertinent of me, but it's vital she's found quickly." George lowered his gaze, lest it give away the truth behind his desperation. "I've got urgent business of my own with her, that can't wait much longer."

Jimmy bent his head to George. "Of course, Mr. Gilmour. It's a constable's duty to help those in need, and you seem to be in need. And, I'm eager to let her know that everything's in place for that poor soul, so

I suppose, in a selfish way, it'd be good if I found her more swiftly, too."

"Thank you, Constable. You can find me at 14 Chandler's Row, when you know more. Or I can come to you—whichever you prefer?" Though he lacked the strength to upturn all of London in pursuit of his daughter, he did not want to put every responsibility upon this man's shoulders. If he could make it easier, in any way, then he would, if only to show his gratitude to this kind Samaritan. "I do not know how I can repay you for this." George gulped; a lump forming in his throat.

Jimmy shook his head. "You don't have to, Mr. Gilmour. It'll be enough for me, to know that Angel's been reunited with her father. I confess, I don't know her well—I mean, truth be told, I don't know her at all—but she seemed like the kind of woman who could use some kindness. When you've walked these streets as often as I have, you get to learn what the looks in people's eyes mean. And she… well, she looked like she had a few ghosts that needed putting to rest."

"Thank you again, Constable. I will look forward to hearing from you." George shook the fellow's hand once more.

"I'll come to you, hopefully with your daughter. If not, I'll come with news," Jimmy promised as George departed the constabulary.

As George stepped out into the brisk air, he gulped down lungful after lungful, as the familiar itch of an insistent cough tickled up his throat.

A moment later, he fell into its grip, his chest wracked with wheezing, spluttering coughs that made his entire body judder under the strain.

Fumbling for his handkerchief, he lifted it to his mouth and tried to ignore the concerned stares of passers-by. All he had to do was battle through it and pray that this would not be the paroxysm that took his life.

A few minutes later, the cough eased, and he managed to draw in a few stable breaths. His body trembled in the aftermath, but that was the least of his worries.

As he took the handkerchief away from his mouth, he glanced down at the white fabric and felt his heart sink. There, spattered across that pale cotton, were spreading pools of crimson. But the sight did not come as a surprise, for it had been this way for weeks now.

I am dying. With each day, Death comes closer to my door. And he did not know how many more days he might have. That was why Angel had to be found quickly, for he did not want to leave this world without hearing her voice one more time, and looking upon her. And, more than that, he did not want to leave this world without letting her know how sorry he was, in the hopes that he might be able to pass into the Kingdom of Heaven with the gift of her forgiveness in his heart.

Chapter Five

Angel could barely keep her head up, as she walked the familiar path along the Thames, towards the Salty Serpent. Even in the dead of night, with only a faint sliver of moonlight to guide her, she knew each step by memory.

She likely could have trodden along in her sleep and made it home all the same, had fatigue claimed her while she was walking.

What time is it? She raised her head slightly to look at the moon, as though it could reply. With a sigh, she pressed on, moving as quickly as her legs could manage.

Now and again, she let her gaze flit to the ever-coursing surface of the river on her right.

It brought her comfort to listen to the subtle sound of it ambling along at its own, steady pace, peppered here and there with the muted clang of a boat on the water, letting others know it was there to avoid collisions in the dark.

There were lights, too, on the boats that did not mind being seen, flickering like eerie will o' the wisps in the gloom. Fishermen and traders and jacks of all trades, making their livelihood from the artery that pulsed all the way from the distant countryside, right into the throbbing heart of London.

Donald will wonder where I am. She sighed, already pre-empting the argument that would occur. Donald did not like interruptions of any kind, where his income was concerned, and the children had been away from their pickpocketing for the whole day.

At least, she hoped they had. For her part, she had stayed at the mortuary until the sun had set and the late evening had turned into the wee hours of the morning again.

A few times, the mortuary workers had tried to urge her to leave, but they'd not had the heart to force her from Solomon's side.

And she simply had not been able to leave him, fearing that, somehow, he might know she had abandoned him.

Only when her tiredness had overwhelmed her, had she finally departed. But not before she had received confirmation from the mortuary that Solomon would, indeed, be buried in a real cemetery, with a stone to mark his grave.

Who on Earth was that constable? She almost wondered if she had imagined him.

Nevertheless, his promise had been real enough. Word had been sent with the mortuary cart that Solomon's body was to be sent to the undertaker in the next day or so, and that all would be paid by this mysterious Constable Milton.

She noted, with some annoyance, that he had not entrusted her with the money he had received from the wealthy passenger of the carriage.

However, she could put her irritation to one side, knowing that Solomon was to be taken care of.

She would make sure of it, by visiting the undertaker herself every day, right until the moment Solomon was interred.

She paused suddenly as a new sound rippled through the silent night. The quiet beat of footsteps, somewhere behind her, moving with some speed.

Swallowing the instant jolt of panic that shot through her, she hurried on at a faster pace.

But her panic came back, tenfold, when the pace of the footsteps also quickened, as though someone were following her.

By now, she knew it was prudent not to be found alone, at night, where nobody would discover her body if something were to happen to her.

There had been enough tragedy for one day, and she did not wish to add herself to the pile.

A second later, she broke into a run. The footsteps matched it, thundering along in the shadows at her back. For a moment, she did not know if they had sped up, or it was merely the rush of blood in her ears.

Either way, she would not risk being wrong. In her eighteen years, she had experienced enough incidents of this ilk to know how to evade people. And this was no different.

Using every tool in her underworld arsenal, she darted into the tangled brush to the side of the riverbank and rushed along on light feet until she reached the looming shapes of nearby warehouses.

There, she slipped down the back of one of the vast structures and crouched low in the darkness behind a cluster of barrels. Through a crack to one side, she peered out, so she might see if the person following her was friend, foe, or neither.

A few moments later, a figure stopped up ahead. He looked around in confusion, setting one hand on his waist as if trying to catch his breath.

Just then, a cloud drifted away from the moon overhead, offering a silvered torchlight with which Angel might see her pursuer's face.

She clamped her hand over her mouth to prevent a gasp of surprise from escaping.

Constable Milton? What is he doing, following me in the darkness like this?

She waited a while longer, until Jimmy passed by, no doubt hoping he would catch up to her some way along the riverbank. Well, he would be sorely disappointed.

The fact was, it worried her to see him there, given his occupation. Having a man of the law so close to the Salty Serpent did not bring her any comfort whatsoever, for such a man could bring down their entire operation. Terror pummelled through her veins, borne of an intense fear for the welfare of the children in her care.

I must hope his intentions are good, and that he didn't follow me for some untoward reason, she told herself. I've got to hope he's half the person I think he is.

He would not have been the first man to attempt to follow her home, though most of those had been for woefully unsavoury purposes.

Perhaps that's why he didn't give me the money. Perhaps he wanted to see me again, so he kept it, meaning I'd have to come to him in order to check that everything had been put in place for Solomon.

Ordinarily, such a thought would have turned her stomach, or irked her. However, when she thought of Jimmy, she found, to her surprise, that she did not find the idea of seeing him again so unpalatable. And that, in turn, made her all the more afraid.

He may have helped her today, far beyond what he had needed to, but she could not allow herself to risk everything on a handsome face, a soothing voice, and a generous gesture.

For a while, she realised, she would have to keep her head down. A message to Jimmy, to ensure all was well with the undertaker's fee, would have to suffice in place of a physical visit. As for the location of Solomon's final resting place—she could gain that from the undertaker himself.

No, she would not put the children in danger for the sake of these new, concerning thoughts in her mind. For not all constables were like him.

And she would not see her orphans dragged away, because she had been foolish enough to feel charmed by a sweet stranger, who had given one of them a gravestone. The others, she knew, would not be so lucky.

Chapter Six

Several days passed, and Angel kept herself to herself, remaining at the Salty Serpent whilst the children went on with their daily work. She knew she could have gone out and avoided Jimmy easily enough, but she did not want to take any unnecessary chances.

She had already sent her letter to him and had informed him to send his reply directly to the undertaker, where she would collect it. Which she had already done, in the early hours of the morning, a couple of days prior.

It had stated that he had paid for everything but had added an insistence that she come to visit with him, as he had something he wanted to talk to her about.

She had yet to respond to that, in any manner.

Indeed, it had almost been three days since she had picked up his reply, when she finally dared to set foot outside again.

She needed to visit with the undertaker one last time, so she could receive the date of Solomon's burial. After all of this, she would not allow him to be buried without her present.

After taking a different route, steering clear of the river path in case Jimmy found her there, Angel was barely fifteen minutes from the undertaker's place of business, when she felt a sharp tug on her hand.

She had been so absorbed in her thoughts that she had not noticed the approach of one of her wards.

"Angel! Angel! You've to come, quick!" Sally, one of the older girls in Donald's employ, yelped in fright.

It took Angel a second to come to her senses. "What's that matter, Sally? Has something happened?" She did not know that she could endure hearing that another of the children had come to harm.

Sally nodded effusively. "It's Leon. He's been caught! I told 'im not to try stealing from one of the merchants, but he didn't listen. Then, I saw you pass by and I had to come tell you! Please, Angel—he needs you!"

"Lead the way," Angel instructed, with a voice calmer than she felt. In truth, she was torn, knowing that if she showed her face to any constable, it might feed back to Jimmy. However, she also knew she could not leave a child to flounder. Not under any circumstance.

Together, Angel and Sally hurried through the streets until they came to a small square, where spindly trees swayed in the cold breeze.

A gentleman in fine clothing stood off to one side with a uniformed constable whom she did not know, the two of them talking animatedly. As her gaze drifted to the other side of the square, her heart sank.

Two more figures stood there, in the midst of an equally animated discussion—one was Leon, and one was Jimmy himself.

Steeling her nerve, she approached with purpose. "Constable Milton, good day to you."

Jimmy's eyes widened. "Angel?"

"I came as soon as I heard that there'd been some unrest," she ploughed on, struggling to hold his gaze. He had such kind eyes, and it made her heart beat in a most unusual way.

"Unrest? I think it's more than that, Angel," Jimmy replied sombrely. "Do you know this boy here?"

Angel nodded, as the lies danced upon the tip of her tongue. "He is one of my wards, at the orphanage where I work. Is he in some kind of trouble?"

"He was caught trying to steal a pocket watch from that man over there." Jimmy gestured to the rich fellow on the opposite side of the square.

"I didn't try to steal nothing!" Leon protested. "He'd dropped his pocket watch and I were trying to give it back."

Angel had heard the same excuse countless times, for it was one of the easiest lies to tell, in order to evade arrest. "Constable Milton, this boy isn't a bad child. He's had a hard life, and I know there are so many others who've had a life just as difficult, but if you arrest him and send him away today, then what chance will he have? Say he is telling the truth—what sort of reward would it be, for him trying to do good, if he gets locked up for it? Let him go, I beg of you, and I'll see to it that he doesn't get himself into any more trouble."

"I can't do that." Jimmy sighed, casting her an expression of regret.

"Then, let him remedy this some other way," she implored. "Speak with the merchant and ask if he'd consider having Leon work for him a while, to make up for any wrongdoing he thinks has been done to him today. See if you can't appeal to him. He'll listen to you, but I doubt he'll listen to me."

There was another reason for Angel's request. Throughout her time working for Donald, she had always done her best to try and find alternative employment for the children there.

A way out of the life she had never been able to escape.

And here, she spotted just such an opportunity for Leon, who had always been industrious. He just needed stability, and Angel felt certain he would flourish.

Jimmy frowned, thinking for a moment. "Wait here. I'll go and speak to him. But don't try to run, else you'll make this worse."

"I won't, I promise." Angel had every intention of running, with the children at her side, if this took a sourer turn. But Jimmy did not need to know that.

As Jimmy walked away, Leon peered up at her. "Do you think he'll say yes?" A curious light of excitement had entered the boy's eyes, filling Angel with hope.

"Would you like him to?" she replied.

The boy shrugged. "I've always looked at the lads who work for the merchants on the docks, and thought it'd be a nice life. They're always laughing, and they're never short of a bob or two. I wouldn't mind it, I don't think." He paused, looking suddenly frightened. "But will Mr. McIntyre let me go?"

"You leave Mr. McIntyre to me," Angel assured. "If the merchant says yes, I'll make sure you can go."

Jimmy came back a few minutes later, with a stunned smile on his face. "Mr. Phelps, the merchant, says he's happy to let the boy work for him, for a time, to make up for his actions. I explained the situation, and might've embellished a bit, but he's said he won't press any charges so long as the boy comes with him now."

"Now?" Angel's heart wrenched.

"Those are the terms. I guess Mr. Phelps is worried that the boy will run off, if he doesn't come along now," Jimmy replied.

"I don't mind!" Leon interjected, with a note of eagerness. "I can go now. I ain't got nothing to bring, so it's not like I need to pack."

Angel mustered a sad chuckle. "No, I suppose that's true."

"Can I, Angel?" Leon pleaded.

What choice do I have? This is your escape route, Leon. Make the most of it. She reached out and held Leon's face in her hands, planting a gentle kiss on top of his forehead.

She had an inkling that this might be the last time she saw him, for once he had escaped this world of pickpocketing and theft, he would have been a fool to return.

"Of course you can," she said softly. "But don't you waste this opportunity, do you hear? You behave, you work hard, and maybe you'll make a great man of yourself one of these days. And, when you do, you come back and tell me all about it.

Leon put his arms around Angel and squeezed her tight.

"Make this Mr. Phelps see that you're a good boy, who can do well. Don't you let me down, you hear?"

"I won't, Angel. I swear it."

"Then... off you go."

Angel gave him a gentle nudge in the right direction, as he took off across the square and went to speak with the finely dressed gentleman. She observed their discussion, though she could not hear what was being said. However, it cheered her to see a small smile appear on the face of Mr. Phelps—a kindly one, that suggested Leon was not walking into unsafe hands.

"Angel, if I could—" Jimmy's voice cut through her private reverie, only to be abruptly interrupted by her own.

"I really must be on my way, Constable Milton. Thank you again for what you have done for me today, and what you have done for me in past days. I have not forgotten it, and I will not forget it."

She took Sally by the hand and turned, leading the girl away at speed. It pained her, to have to leave Leon so swiftly, but she could not risk getting into any further conversation with Jimmy.

Her mind was already in turmoil where he was concerned, and though Leon had been fortunate today, she still had so many others to think of.

She had, however, underestimated Jimmy's determination to speak with her.

He had his mission from George Gilmour weighing heavy upon his mind, and though wrangling Angel into staying in one place for long enough to tell her she was being looked for had been proving a near-impossible task, he was not the sort of fellow to give up so easily.

You are a remarkable woman, Angel.

There were not many who would have done what she had done today, turning a dire circumstance into one of optimism.

Still, he could tell she was worried about something more than she would let on, but that only made him all the more motivated to fulfil his promise and unite her with her father.

He had a good sense when it came to people, and he had been able to tell that George was a sincere, respectable sort of man. A father who mourned a bygone separation.

And, perhaps, Angel was a daughter who mourned the loss of a father. If George had been looking for her, for so long, then it stood to reason that Angel did not even know he was alive. Jimmy hoped to remedy that, if he could just get her to listen.

He waited a minute, before following Angel at a discreet distance. Meanwhile, she pressed on, seemingly oblivious to his presence.

Though he had constabulary duties to attend to, he trailed Angel and the little girl at her side all the way along the river path, past the same warehouses where he had lost sight of her the other night, and on until they reached a dilapidated ship, nestled into the side of the muddied bank.

He ducked behind a nearby tree and peered out, curious as to why they had suddenly stopped.

He understood, a moment later, when the two of them disappeared into the wrecked vessel.

This is where she lives? It baffled him, for it looked like nothing more than an empty husk. Truthfully, he had not believed her when she had mentioned she worked at an orphanage.

It was just something about her anxious demeanour, although it would have made some logical sense, considering her attachment to the poor boy who had died in the street, and her insistence upon helping the one who had almost had himself arrested.

But this reality of where she was living confused him all the more. Why would such a woman live in a dire place like this? And how was it that she came to know so many dejected children?

He contemplated going after her, to retrieve answers to all of his questions, but stopped short. If he pursued her now, he would only frighten her away.

No, he would bide his time, and find a way to speak with her alone. Now that he knew where she resided, it would be much easier to 'accidentally' cross paths with her, and make sure she listened this time.

It may not be as swift as you wanted, Mr. Gilmour, but I'll bring her back to you... I swear it. Unfortunately for Jimmy, he did not realise the gravity of George's situation. For Angel's father, time was quickly running out.

Chapter Seven

Angel stood alone at Solomon's open graveside, tears ravaging her cheeks. The afternoon had turned bitterly cold, with an ominous sky overhead that threatened snow.

She drew her knitted scarf tighter around her neck, though she could no longer feel any sensation in her cheeks or hands, no matter how deep she pushed the latter into her pockets.

She tried to find some kind of peace as she stood there, staring down at the plain wooden casket that lay within.

A woefully small one, for a grave so large it seemed to swamp the coffin.

She mouthed a silent prayer, to send Solomon on his way, struggling to ignore the chatter of the nearby gravediggers as she did so. They loitered off to one side, leaning on their shovels, complaining about the frost-hardened ground.

"Do you mind?" she said coldly, lifting her gaze.

The gravediggers scowled and fell silent.

I'm sorry I couldn't get you out, Solomon. She thought of Leon, who had seamlessly vanished into his new life.

Donald had not been too pleased about the boy's separation from the pickpocketing gang, but Angel had done her best to try and placate him, explaining that it had been the only way to keep Leon from prison.

Naturally, Donald had muttered about retrieving the boy, once his term of service was finished with the merchant he had tried to rob, but Angel felt certain that her employer would forget in due course and Leon would be able to escape his former life for good. And not in the manner that Solomon had.

As she continued to stand vigil, she wondered just how many more of these children she would lose before she, herself, found a way out?

Too many… People from this world rarely made it out alive.

***

Weary from the solitary service that commemorated Solomon's short life, Angel returned to the Salty Serpent in something of a daze.

Her head ached from dehydration, having shed so many tears for the poor boy.

In truth, all she wanted was her bed, and some time to come to terms with her grief.

Not that she would be permitted such a luxury.

There were children to wrangle and food to cook, and Donald would not tolerate any slacking, not for any reason.

I'll need to beg more coal for the fire, she reminded herself as she ambled along the river path.

The first few flakes of snow had begun to fall, landing upon her face with an icy kiss.

It was another concern of her daily life, that she would awaken to find that one or more of the children had died of exposure in their sleep.

That was the trouble with living where they lived; the wrecked ship was open to the elements, the wind whistling and howling through the cracks in the planks at all hours of the day and night, which no amount of stuffing with fabric could remove.

And when it rained, it poured within the ship, too.

Droplets splashing the floorboards, trickling tributaries worming down the walls and prompting the wood to rot and warp, and gushing torrents cascading down from the ruined deck above, which even buckets could not contain.

She had reached the curve in that path that signalled the final approach to the ship, when a figure emerged from a thicket of wiry trees that rustled to her right. She recoiled in alarm, until she saw his face.

"Constable Milton?" she gasped, resisting the urge to let her eyes dart towards the ship. *Did he follow me the other day? Does he know where I live?*

Panic coursed through her veins, dulling the brief moment of relief she had felt upon seeing him. And the faint flicker of excitement that had come with it.

"Angel." He bowed his head to her. "I hoped I might find you here."

She gulped. "Why would you think that?"

"Because you're here," he said, with a half smile. "And, because I knew you would be returning from Solomon's burial."

"Returning to where?" She had to know what he knew.

He gave a slight shrug. "I was informed that you lived somewhere around here, and that you preferred to walk along the river path. So, I thought it'd be prudent to wait in this spot, since it forks towards every possible path."

He gestured to the crossroads where the path split, heading north, south, and west. To the east lay the river itself.

"Oh…" So, he did not know that she resided aboard the dilapidated vessel in the water, barely one hundred paces from where she stood?

At least, he did not appear to. If he did, then he was exceedingly good at pretending otherwise.

"I don't mean to frighten you, Angel, and I don't mean you any harm. I'd have come to the cemetery instead, but I thought you'd prefer to say your goodbyes on your own, without me interrupting."

He dipped his chin to his chest in a shy action. "However, there's something I need to talk to you about. Not here, and not now, whilst you're still in the throes of sadness, but it's not something that can wait much longer. Would tomorrow suit?"

She frowned. "What's the nature of it?"

"I can't disclose that here. You need to promise me that you'll take a walk with me tomorrow—in Hyde Park, perhaps?" He looked up at her in earnest. "I'm not trying to toy with you. I really do have news that you'll want to hear, which might be of great importance to you. I'm certain you won't regret taking a walk with me, when I tell you what I have to."

"Then why not tell me now?" Angel pressed, confused as to what he might wish to tell her.

"Because there's someone else who wants to be there," Jimmy replied

"Someone who's eager to meet you."

"Who?" Angel squinted at him.

"I can't say, as of yet. Tomorrow, I'll reveal everything. Please, Angel, say you'll be there."

He paused. "We can meet by the Serpentine, where the chestnut sellers usually have their carts?"

"You'll not take no for an answer, will you?" She mustered a sigh, though the idea of meeting with Jimmy in a much more intimate setting did not entirely appeal her, it gave her a fleeting thrill which she quickly forced herself to push down.

She could not feel any such emotions for a constable—not now, not ever. It went against everything she had become.

Jimmy shook his head. "I'm afraid not."

"Very well," she relented. "I'll meet you by the chestnut sellers tomorrow. Does noon fit into your scheme?"

Jimmy gave a quiet laugh. "There's no scheme, Angel, but noon would suit just fine."

"Then tomorrow at noon it is." Her lips curved up into a smile, despite herself. When it came to Jimmy and his kind eyes, she could not help it.

***

Donald McIntyre crouched low behind the bulwark of the Salty Serpent, his ears pricked as he eavesdropped upon the furtive conversation taking place on the bank up ahead. Their voices carried on the faint, cold breeze.

Who is this constable? Donald's eyes narrowed in suspicion, for he had heard Angel address him as Constable Milton. He loathed all men of the law, for they threatened his very existence, and the tidy fortune that he had amassed for himself. Right now, he sensed danger on the wind, mingling with those voices.

This fellow is not to be trusted. Angel is young, and she is foolish—she doesn't realise the peril she's in. That's why she's fortunate she has me, watching over her.

He smiled grimly, a plan forming in his mind which would kill two birds with one stone—literally, if all went well. If this constable thought he could walk into Angel's life, and take her away from him, then he had another thing coming. In truth, Donald had more selfish reasons for being concerned about the arrival of this young, handsome gentleman in uniform.

He did not intend to let any man have her, other than himself. He had worked too hard, moulding her into the woman he desired, above all others.

And she knew much too much to ever be released from his grasp.

You won't interfere in my plan to wed her and have her for myself. Nor will you intervene in my business, One and the same they are, one and the same.

Donald McIntyre was well aware that the business could not continue without Angel's aid, and he did not intend to give up his income.

Donald glowered at the constable for a moment longer, before he drew away from the bulwark and crept downstairs. There, he found Jack—an older boy of three-and-ten, who had become one of Donald's most prolific and trusted employees.

"Jack, I've a job for you," Donald said, without preamble.

Jack frowned. "What can I do, Mr. McIntyre?"

"Follow Angel to Hyde Park, tomorrow at noon. There, you'll see her with a young gentleman in a constable's uniform. That fellow intends to do her harm, Jack, and I won't allow that to happen. He's blackmailing her, and we've got to stop him, for her sake."

Donald stretched the truth of what he actually knew. "I'll give you the tools to see the job done. All you've got to do is make sure he doesn't exit that park alive; do you understand?"

Jack hesitated. "Someone's trying to hurt Angel?"

They all adore her. They'd do anything for her. Just as he had known they would. That was why he had chosen the tale that he had, for he knew it was the only thing that could encourage a child to kill someone in cold blood.

"They are, Jack. They'll lock her up and throw away the key, if we don't help her. Will you do it, Jack?" Donald waited patiently, already knowing what the answer would be.

A moment later, Jack nodded. "For Angel, I will. You can count on me."

Donald grinned. "I knew I could."

Chapter Eight

Angel stole away from the Salty Serpent the following morning and made the lengthy walk from her home on the riverbank to the green expanse of Hyde Park.

She often came here in the summertime, when the trees were full of emerald leaves and the warm sunshine enveloped her in its balmy embrace. In the depths of winter, however, the scene proved much less inviting.

The trees had lost their summer plumage, the last remnants of the dead leaves turning to mulch upon the intersecting pathways that ran through the park.

Still, she pressed on with her collar turned up to her chin, until she came to the thoroughfare where the roasted chestnut sellers were hawking their wares.

Jimmy awaited her there, with a paper bag filled with the silken-shelled chestnuts. "I was worried you might not come."

"You didn't leave me with much choice," she replied, not unkindly. On the long walk here, she had found her stomach churning with a new kind of anxiety—the errant flutter of butterflies in her abdomen. And she knew, without a shadow of a doubt, that Jimmy was to blame.

"Would you like one?" He offered her a chestnut.

"Be rude not to." She took one and tossed it between her hands to cool it down, before taking a tentative bite. It burned her tongue, as she had known it would, but she did not mind. It was part of the winter ritual of eating these sweet delights.

The nutty, smoky, sugary flavour of the chestnut emerged from the initial burn, reminding her of childhood walks with her father. She paused, the nut held between her fingers as though she were a squirrel, as sadness struck her out of nowhere.

She had forgotten about the walks she had taken with her father in this park. Her father had always bought a bag for them to share, whilst they wandered around the park at their leisure. Having very little money to spare, it was a treat that she had always looked forward to. But Angel had long ago pushed those memories from her mind for the pain they caused. But now they resurfaced and brought that pain to her features.

"Angel?" Jimmy peered at her in concern. "Don't you like the taste?"

She swallowed her mouthful. "I like the taste very much."

"Then... is something else wrong?"

She forced a smile onto her lips. "Not at all. It just burned my tongue."

"They do that." He chuckled, and it transformed the false smile into one a touch more genuine. "Shall we walk?"

"I thought we were meeting someone else?" Angel looked around, expecting the mysterious person to appear.

Jimmy grimaced. "He couldn't make it, unfortunately, but I'll explain everything as we walk."

"Very well." Her brow furrowed in thought, wondering if this had all been a ruse to get her alone. She supposed she would find out in due course. And it was not as though she had any other plans that afternoon. What harm was there in a walk?

Over the course of the next half an hour, Jimmy did not reveal the details of why he had asked her here, but Angel found she did not mind the delay.

They strolled and talked about their lives, with Angel bending the truth somewhat to conceal the nature of her employ, and settled into a comfortable companionship which caught her by surprise, and she was rather taken aback by how pleasant this entire encounter was proving to be.

Angel had forgotten the simple pleasure of walking and talking with someone, and learning more of who they were, and what they enjoyed in life. In the same vein, she had forgotten how nice it felt to tell someone of herself, and her own enjoyments.

Spending all of her time around children had given her little cause for prolonged interaction with other adults, with the exception of Donald—but one could only bear the same face for so long, without it becoming a tiresome endeavour to converse with them.

He's got charm, I'll grant him that. He had spoken of an idyllic sounding childhood on the outskirts of London, in the countryside, where he had helped his father on the family farm.

But he had not been without his tragedies. His father had died some years before with a vast amount of debt, meaning the farm had been seized by the debt collectors, leaving Jimmy without any inheritance to speak of.

Nevertheless, he had been determined to make something of himself, for his mother's sake.

He had been a voluntary constable in his township, but had sought to make a greater difference, which had prompted him to come here to London, to become a legitimate man of the law.

At the end of every month, he returned home for a day, to give half of his pay to his mother and visit with her. And, with every word of his tale, Angel found herself all the more enchanted by this man.

"That must be why you're different from the others, then," Angel said aloud, without realising.

"Pardon?" Jimmy glanced at her.

She flushed slightly. "You didn't grow up in London, so it didn't have the chance to harden you. That must be why you're not as ruthless and uncaring as the other constables I've come across."

"You've encountered a lot of us?" he teased.

She shrugged. "My fair share. It's impossible not to, when you come from lowly stock."

"There's nothing lowly about you." His eyes glittered with warmth, making her feel funny.

This is absurd. How could she find pleasure in his company, considering she was a thief, and he was a constable? And yet, the truth would not be denied.

She could not help it.

Being near him soothed her in a way nothing had, since she had been under the protection of her father. At Jimmy's side, she felt... safe. And safety had been hard to come by these last ten years. It was likely why she had never dared to leave Donald's employ, for it was the closest thing to security she had managed to find, albeit tenuous.

"I've embarrassed you," Jimmy apologised.

Angel laughed. "It takes more than a compliment to embarrass me, Constable."

"So, how is it that you've come to be the saviour of so many children?" Jimmy segued awkwardly into a change of topic, which suggested that he was the one suffering from embarrassment.

"Didn't I tell you?" She wracked her brain, trying to remember what tale she had told him previously.

"You mentioned something about an orphanage, but you weren't specific," he prompted.

She was about to answer with a swift lie, when she noticed one of the boys, Jack, from the Salty Serpent standing in the shadow of the trees up ahead.

A man she did not recognise stood at his side, and Angel did not like the look of him at all. He was broad and thick set, with a tangle of red hair and a pair of grim, dark eyes which, fortunately, were not focused on her.

It was not unusual for the children from the ship to run errands for Donald, and the two of them did seem to be muttering to one another, but something about their demeanour made her chest grip in a vice of concern.

Donald couldn't know about this. I was careful... very careful. She had behaved as she always did, the previous evening, preparing a hearty meal for the inhabitants of their home. Well, as hearty as she could, with the meagre provisions she had at her disposal.

She had even stayed up with Donald, by the fire, and listened to him chatter away for hours upon hours as he drank the better half of a bottle of brandy.

He had never given any indication that he thought something was amiss, and she had slipped away from the ship under the pretence of going to purchase some of the excess food shipments that came into the docks.

Shrugging it off as paranoia, and turning her head so that Jack and the other man would not see her, she guided Jimmy away from those trees and turned him down a different path.

I am forever on-edge! I have to learn that not everyone is a threat, she scolded herself.

It was her perpetual state—always on alert for this and that, unable to relax, even for a moment. This walk had been the closest thing to leisure she had enjoyed in a long time. And she felt somewhat peeved that Jack and the red-haired fellow had ruined her peace with their presence.

"So, what did you want to tell me?"

Angel knew her time here was running short, and she did not want to leave without the information he had promised. It had been a wonderful walk, up until that moment, but she would not be satisfied until she had uncovered the secret of his asking her here.

"Ah, yes. I'd almost forgotten." Jimmy smiled and opened his mouth to speak. He did not get any further, however, as a small figure darted around her and skidded to a halt right in front of them.

Angel jumped in fright, clasping a hand to her heart. "Sally! You scared me half to death!"

The little girl looked pale, as if she, too, had received a terrible fright. "You're in trouble, Angel."

"What?" Angel leant forward and held Sally by the shoulders. "Tell me what you mean, Sally."

The little girl went up on tiptoe, to whisper in Angel's ear. "Your friend 'ere—the one who helped Leon—he's in danger. Mr. McIntyre found out where you was going, and he wants to hurt the constable. He thinks the constable wants to ruin us and wants to steal you away. I overheard him talking with Jack early this mornin', while you was making 'is tea, tellin' him to meet with one of his associates here. I 'ad to come and tell you. I know the constable's a good man, even if he wears that uniform. I didn't want to see anything bad happen to 'im, after what he did for Leon. You need to get 'im out of here, now!"

"Go to the flower-seller by St. Paul's and tell her I sent you. Tell her you need somewhere safe to stay, and I'll come and get you as soon as I can. If Donald finds out what you've told me, I don't know what he might do." Angel first thought of the little girl, who'd put herself in harm's way to come and say all of this.

Sally nodded. "You'll come back for me, though, won't you?" Her lip trembled; her eyes wide in panic.

"I swear it," Angel promised. "Now, go." Sally took off without another word, leaving Angel to think of a way to get Jimmy out of here. "We have to leave. We're not safe here. We have to go, immediately!"

Jimmy took her by the hand. "What's wrong? Is someone trying to hurt you?"

"Not me, Jimmy." She stared deep into his eyes. "You. And it's all my fault. I was followed. Please, you have to get out of here now!"

"I'm not leaving you, if you're in—" Jimmy's words died on his lips as the redhaired brute barrelled into him. Angel had hesitated too long.

"Get off him!" she yelped, plunging into the fray. But the muscular philistine was much too strong for her. With a swipe of his hand, he threw her off him, sending her crashing into the ground with a thud that rendered her breathless.

As she struggled to haul herself to her feet, she looked upon Jimmy in horror.

The redhaired cretin sat astride the constable, and his meaty, foul fists were pummelling into the poor young man's face and chest and throat—wherever he could land a blow, he did.

Jimmy tried to fight back, but the wretch had his arms pinned down under the might of his knees, immobilising him.

All Jimmy could do was lie there as the brute beat the life out of him, whilst blood poured from his mouth and his nose, and the first swells of bruises began to bloom beneath his skin.

"No!" Angel cried, stumbling towards the assailant. She grabbed at his red hair, yanking hard, but the wretch barely seemed to feel it. A moment later, he punched her hard in the stomach, making her tumble back onto the dirt. She lay there, blinking up at the grey sky in vacant surprise, as pain ricocheted through her body.

Get up! Get up! Obeying her internal screams, she twisted around and began the slow crawl towards Jimmy, who had gone entirely still.

Just then, whistles pierced the air and the attacker looked up sharply. Constables had appeared at the far end of the path, and they were running fast towards their comrade.

Instantly, the brute leapt up and sprinted away, his knuckles scraped and dripping with the crimson of Jimmy's blood. Still, Angel did not stop in her crawl towards Jimmy.

She had to reach him. She had to make sure he was alive. She could not lose him, when she had only just begun to get to know him.

"Jimmy?" she rasped, collapsing at his side.

His head turned painfully slowly. "Angel..."

"I'm here. I'm here."

He coughed, sending more blood spattering down his chin. "I'm sorry I put... you in... danger."

"You didn't, Jimmy. Goodness, you didn't. I was the one who put you in danger." She lifted her hand to his face, not caring about the slick blood that covered every inch of his skin. "Just stay with me, now. Do you hear? You stay with me!"

Don't let him die... please, don't let him die!

His eyes watered with tears. "It's getting... dark, Angel."

"No, it's not. It's daylight, and you're going to live. You've got to stay with me!" she begged.

"I'm sorry," he wheezed. "I should've told you... the truth."

"Don't you worry about that now. You can tell me when you're better," she said, stroking his cheek.

He grimaced in pain. "It can't... wait." A gurgle escaped his throat, breaking Angel's heart. "It's... your father. I... know where he... is."

With that, unconsciousness claimed him. And Angel's world shattered beneath her.

Chapter Nine

Night fell upon the hospital room where Jimmy lay still, seemingly lifeless to those who might pass by his bed. Angel had not moved from her seat at his side, from the moment he had been brought here by his colleagues, watching day blend into darkness.

The trio of constables who had come to Jimmy's aid had questioned who she was and why she wished to follow Jimmy to the hospital, as though she were part of some interrogation.

However, they had soon let her be, when they realised the depth of her distress. She did not cry easily, but the tears had not ceased in all the hours she had been here.

Only someone who cared could be so distraught. And Angel did care, though it surprised her as much as anyone.

"Please wake up," she said softly, for the millionth time. Her hand clung to his in desperation, not only for his welfare but for the secret that he had only just managed to gasp out before he had fallen into oblivion. "Jimmy? Can you hear me?"

The silence was deafening.

"I need you to wake up, Jimmy," she went on, undeterred. "I need you to wake up, so I can see you are all right. I need you to wake up, so you can tell me where my father is. I need you to wake up, so that I can..." She trailed off, for she did not dare to say what was on her mind. *I need you to wake up, so that I can continue to care for you... if you will allow me.*

These past ten years, she had never had the liberty of having something that was entirely her own.

She had never given a single thought to falling in love, or finding a good man to marry, or breaking away from Donald's control. Somehow, without her realising, Jimmy had changed all of that.

She did not know if the fluttering in her stomach was love, as of yet, but she had an inkling that it could turn into something wonderful.

Yet, here he lay, pummelled half to death by a brute that Donald had sent. And she did not know if he would ever wake up. Once again, Donald had stolen her freedom from her.

"Miss?" One of the orderlies approached, with a nervous manner about him.

She peered up at him. "Yes?"

"You've got to leave, Miss. You can't be staying here through the night. I'd let you, if I could, but I've been told to tell you to go."

Her face crumpled. "I have to stay with him."

"You can't, Miss. You can come back tomorrow, but you can't stay here tonight. You've to be on your way." He paused, casting his gaze down towards the floor. "I'm sorry."

She noticed two more men, far more robust than this messenger, standing in the doorway at the end of the ward.

She supposed they intended to physically remove her, if she did not obey.

Ordinarily, she would have fought until they allowed her to remain, but she had other business to attend to, that would not wait.

Donald could not be allowed to get away with what he had done, and she planned to let him know just what she thought of him—words that ought to have been spoken a long time ago.

Moreover, come the morning, she knew she would have to make a detour to the flower-seller before she came back here, to make sure that a safe sanctuary could be found for Sally.

That brave, bold little girl had risked everything for Jimmy, and for her, and Angel would not forget it. Even if it cost her every penny she had managed to hide away, she would see Sally free and happy.

Turning her attention back to Jimmy, she lifted his hand to her lips and kissed it gently. "I'll come back for you tomorrow, Jimmy. I've not left you. If I'm not here when you wake up, please know that I haven't abandoned you. I'm coming back, I swear it." She glanced at the orderly. "Will you tell him I stayed, if he wakes before I return?"

The orderly nodded. "I will. What name should I give him?"

"Tell him that Angel didn't leave his side, until she was forced to. And tell him that Angel is going to come back, to sit right here with him, until he's better," she replied firmly.

"Angel?" He frowned, as though he did not quite believe it to be her real name.

"That's me." She kissed Jimmy's hand again, before rising from her chair.

She might have been eager to remain with Jimmy, but she would not suffer the indignity of being kicked out of this hospital by those two burly men who continued to linger.

"Then, I'll make sure he knows, if he wakes up."

Angel's breath hitched. "If?"

"I meant "when." Sorry. It's just a turn of phrase." The orderly looked embarrassed, but the damage had already been done.

Evidently, nobody expected Jimmy to survive his devastating injuries. Nobody but Angel. She would not give up hope… not yet. Until she had to bury him in the ground, she would not believe that death was coming for him.

The orderly followed her down the main aisle of the ward and did not leave her until she was out in the cold night air. It irked her, to have to endure an escort, as though she were a common criminal, but she held her tongue.

She needed these people to think her harmless, for when she returned. If they suspected she might be trouble, she knew they would not allow her to set foot inside the building again.

I'm coming back, Jimmy. You wait and see. And, when I do, I promise I won't leave again. I won't lie again. I'll tell you everything, and I'll hope that you can overlook it, and I'll hope that what I've been feeling isn't just a fleeting figment of my imagination. Glancing back at the hospital once more, she turned on her heel and set off for the Salty Serpent.

***

The moment she stepped under the low lintel of the main room of the wrecked ship, she found Donald waiting for her.

He paced the floor, a glass of brandy in hand, and when he looked up at her, she could sense the anger bristling out of his every vile pore.

She only hoped that he could sense her anger, for she had never been so livid and disgusted in all her young life.

"How could you?" she hissed. "What harm had that man caused to you? None! He did not mean me any ill-will, and you had someone beat him to within an inch of his life!"

"Don't you dare." Donald glowered at her. "Don't you dare try and blame me for this, Angel. You brought this on yourself, fraternising with a man of the law! What choice did you leave me, huh? You're a fool. A fool who put us all in danger, because you had your eye caught by some handsome dolt in a uniform!"

Rage jabbed at her chest. "I did no such thing, you selfish, ignorant wretch! That 'handsome dolt' had news about my father, and he was about to tell me everything when your man tried to punch him to dust!" She stormed right up to him, her face close to his.. "This had nothing to do with you, or your business. Do you think I'd do anything to put the children in harm's way? I love them all more than I love anything in this world!"

"More than me?" His breath stank of alcohol.

"Of course, more than you! I don't give two hoots about you! Why would I, when you've done nothing but trap me here?" she yelled, swiping the brandy glass out of his hand. It hit the floor and smashed into a thousand glittering shards, spilling the remaining liquid onto the wooden boards, where it dripped down through the rot and filth.

His cheeks turned crimson with fury. "Trapped you here? I've given you everything!" His hand shot out and grasped her by the wrist. "But if it's trapped you want, then it's trapped ye'll get! Maybe some time alone will make you see what an idiot you've been. Maybe a bit of solitary confinement will bring you to your senses!"

She tried to dig her heels into the ground as he wrenched her forward, dragging her through the dilapidated ship until they reached the door to one of the storage cupboards—used for hiding all the bulkier items that the children brought in.

With her free hand, she pounded at his chest and his side and his back, but he did not react. Instead, he drew back the bolt on the storage cupboard and threw open the door. A moment later, he hurled her inside with such strength that she careened into the far wall.

It took her a second too long to regain her balance. By the time she'd run for the door, to try and get away, it slammed in her face.

"Let me out!" she screamed, battering the surface with her fists.

"You need to learn a lesson, m'girl!" he shouted back. "You need to learn not to bite the hand that feeds you!"

"You let me out, this minute!" Angel banged harder on the door, until her hands ached.

The sound of retreating footsteps echoed back, but she would not give up until she had escaped that tyrant and his miserable ship.

"Children?! Children, can you hear me?! Let me out, I beg of you! Let me out of here!" She tried a different tactic, to no avail. No further footsteps thudded in the corridor beyond.

She could not even hear the slightest squeak of someone coming to her aid, and she knew why.

Although the children adored her, they feared Donald. And, right now, their fear was stronger.

No-one is coming to help me, she realised.

From here-on-in, she did not know what might happen to her, or Jimmy, or her father, or Sally. Now, she really was trapped.

Chapter Ten

Jimmy stirred wearily to dimly lit surroundings that he did not recognise. He sensed he was lying down somewhere and tried to get a better view of his location, but something obscured his vision. He struggled to blink, but his eyes did not cooperate, and the interference in his view did not clear.

He gently touched his swollen eyes. Through them, he had only a sliver of sight with which to see by. However, from his present angle, he could not see much at all, aside from a shadowed ceiling overhead.

This would not do. No, this would not do at all, for he did not like to be vulnerable in any situation.

Especially when he could not quite remember what had befallen him. Determined, he tried to move, only to be overwhelmed by a surging wave of absolute pain.

I'm hurt… badly hurt. A hazy recollection came back to him, of a furious demon with flying fists, battering him senseless. He thought he remembered Angel being there, but the memory evaded him—just out of his reach. If she had been with him then, she was not with him now. That much, he knew.

Was she injured? Did that devil try to hurt her, too? No matter how he tried, he could not get his mind, nor his body, to cooperate. He shifted again, to try and find a more comfortable position, when a sound distracted him. A soft, furtive whispering somewhere nearby, beyond the limited boundaries of his vision. He paused and lay still, listening closer to the unusual noise.

"Are you sure that's him? It'll cost you, if it ain't." A gruff, masculine voice spoke, in that hushed tone.

"I swear it's him. Constable Jimmy Milton, right? That's the man you're after?" a second, less powerful voice replied.

"Aye, Constable Milton. That's the one I were sent to deal with." The first man sighed. "Here's your pay. Don't you breathe a word of this, else you'll suffer. I know your face now, and if word of my being here gets out, I'll know who to come for."

"I won't say a word!" the second man squeaked.

"You best not." A strange, unsettling scrape of metal pierced the quietude. "This'll be over with soon, so I suggest you make yourself scarce."

"Of course." With the scuffle of hurrying footsteps, Jimmy guessed that the second man had obeyed and made a run for it. Which meant that Jimmy was in serious danger.

He had heard that same, metallic sound many times before, and knew it to be the scrape of a blade against a flint, to sharpen it. Someone had been sent to finish the job. They were going to try and kill him.

Instinct kicked in and he pretended to lie entirely still as heavier footsteps approached his bedside. He had the element of surprise, and he did not plan to lose it.

Lying there, he bided his time, letting his other senses take over.

His ears followed his would-be murderer's footfalls across the hospital floor and knew when the man had come to a standstill to the right of his bed. In the ensuing silence, he heard the man's ragged breaths. A moment later, Jimmy heard the strain of fabric and the subtle shift in the air as his assassin raised his arm.

He waited until the very last moment before he wrenched his body sideways, yanking hard on the bedframe to pull himself over the edge.

He landed with a thud on the floor, just in time to see a blade plunge into the now-vacant mattress where his chest had been, not a moment ago.

With all the strength he could muster, he used the same bedframe to haul himself to his feet. An entire bed provided a barrier between Jimmy and the murderer, but Jimmy knew that would only deter the man for a couple of seconds. If that.

"You won't learn when to die, will you?" the stranger seethed.

He stood at over six feet, with a surprisingly lithe frame, and a set of glinting eyes that sparked in the darkness. A far cry from the meaty brute who had first made an attempt on Jimmy's life.

The assassin leapt up onto the mattress with athletic grace, whilst Jimmy staggered back into the bed behind him.

"I won't die at your hand," Jimmy shot back, fumbling for the pillow of the bed to his back. He lifted it at precisely the right moment, the blade of the murderer's knife sinking harmlessly through the down within and cutting right through to the other side, inches from Jimmy's face.

Using everything he had learned during his time with the London Constabulary, Jimmy twisted the pillow and tugged it away to the left, taking the knife with it.

He threw the pillow as far as he could, grunting against the agony that pounded through his veins, and watched as it disappeared beneath a bed opposite. He had managed to remove the potential murder weapon, but Jimmy knew that would not save him.

"You're a tricky one. I'll give you that. But you'll die, either way." The assassin jumped towards him like a tiger pouncing.

Jimmy, however, was ready for him, already pre-empting what the attacker would do.

Howling against the pain that seared through him, he ducked out of the way of the assailant and twisted back around, grappling the wiry fellow around the neck.

He clamped his arm around the attacker's throat with everything he possessed, and dragged him down onto the nearest bed.

The assailant may have been thin, but the weight of him against Jimmy's chest proved to be almost crushing. Jimmy supposed he'd taken some injuries to his torso, and the smallest pressure had exacerbated the situation, but still he refused to let go of his would-be murderer.

In fact, he held on like his life depended on it. Which, it did. He held on with the hope of seeing Angel again. And he held on, for the sake of his mother, who had already lost so much... she did not need to add the death of her only child to her life's struggles.

The attacker flailed and writhed and wriggled, like a fish on a hook, but Jimmy only clamped down harder with the crook of his arm. And he did not release his grip until, after a few minutes, his assailant went entirely limp.

Even then, he held on for a short while longer, just in case the attacker was merely pretending to be unconscious.

His breathing has changed, Jimmy realised. The man's inhalations had grown short and shallow—the kind that could not be falsified.

Satisfied that he had managed to render the fiend unconscious, Jimmy rolled the wretch away and slithered out from under him. On shaky legs, Jimmy staggered away from the bed, using the frame to hold himself up. He continued on along the main aisle of the hospital ward, using the rest of the frames to steady his course, until he reached the doorway. There, he paused, and peered out through his limited vision.

The hallway beyond lay empty. Likely, so that no-one would be around to witness the murder of a constable.

I'm not safe here. I have to get out... I have to find Angel. He slipped out of the door and made his way along the hallway, sliding along the wall so he would not stumble and fall.

He carried on in that fashion until he had reached the entrance, where he hobbled out into the bitter cold of the night.

Only then did he realise that he wore naught but his open shirt and the trousers he had donned that morning, his coat and uniform jacket having been removed.

With trembling fingertips, he battled with his buttons in a vain attempt to stay the icy air that bit into his skin.

"Constable Milton?" a small, shy voice emerged from the darkness in front of the hospital.

He stared into the shadows. "Who's there?"

A little figure emerged—one he vaguely recognised as the young girl who had come running in Hyde Park, minutes before that vile brute had landed his first blow. "My name's Sally, Constable. I don't know if you remember me from the park? I come to warn you an Angel. And... I'm afraid she might be in trouble."

"Trouble? What kind of trouble?" Jimmy observed the little girl, trying to decipher if she was friend or foe.

"She told me to go somewhere safe, after I come to warn you. I... didn't listen. I wanted to make sure you were both all right." Sally lowered her gaze, shamefaced. "I followed her 'ere and waited outside. She stayed with you until they made 'er leave. After that, I followed 'er back to... uh, where we live. Or, where I used to live. There's a man there, called Donald McIntyre. He's locked 'er up, Constable. And I don't know what he's going to do to 'er. I came back 'ere, hopin' you might wake up, so you could get some other constables to go and save 'er. But the people here wouldn't let me in, and they said you weren't awake yet, so I waited out 'ere. I thought, maybe, I'd be able to sneak in, when they wasn't looking."

Jimmy made the decision to trust her, and prayed his instincts were not wrong. "Come with me, Sally. We will go and rally some other constables, and we will go and free Angel."

He had brushed with death twice that day, and yet it was not his welfare that he cared about. No, Angel was all that mattered, for he had made a promise to her father, and he would not let either of them down, whilst he still had breath left in his body.

Chapter Eleven

Sunlight peeped through the cracks in the structure of the storage cupboard, where the wooden walls had warped and stretched. The faint slices of illumination were a welcome sight to the huddled figure in the corner.

Without them, Angel would not have known what time of day it was, for she had drifted in and out of a fitful slumber since Donald had locked her in here.

She had thudded against the door with her fists until her knuckles bled and fatigue had taken over, forcing her to retreat to the floor, where she had drawn her knees to her chin and prayed for morning.

I shouldn't have come back. I should've stayed away. I shouldn't have allowed my anger to overwhelm me.

She lay her head against the damp wall, mourning her predicament. Jimmy was out there, beyond this ship, and she did not know if he was alive or dead.

Nor did she know what he had been intending to tell her about her father's whereabouts. Perhaps, her father was dead, too.

Just then, the sound of the bolt scraping back splintered through the dull quiet. Angel sank back further against the wall as the door opened and Donald filled the frame.

He held a lantern in his hand, and wasted no time in stepping inside, whilst ensuring he closed the door behind him. In his other hand, he held a long stick. No doubt, he intended to strike her with it, if she attempted to escape.

"I hope you're feeling calmer this morning?" he said acidly.

She said nothing in reply, not trusting the venom that formed upon her tongue.

"You know you made me do this, Angel. I will do anything to protect my livelihood, and your stupid actions might've put us all in peril. But I will forgive you, because I love you." He shone the lantern in her face. "You've toyed with me long enough, Angel. You wounded me, when I saw you with that constable. But I'm not about to have you taken away from me, not by anyone. As such, I've removed the problem. You don't need to worry about that constable anymore—he has been dealt with. Now, we can be together."

Angel's stomach plummeted. "What do you mean?"

"I mean, there's nothing standing in our way anymore. The constable is no more, and you owe me for your mistake." He leered at her in the gloom, and she hugged her legs tighter.

"He... is dead?"

Tears sprang to her eyes, for she knew that she was to blame. If she had stayed away, as she ought to have done, then he would be alive. Donald would never have noticed him and sought revenge upon him. "But... he was only trying to help me, Donald. He wanted to tell me about my father. There wasn't anything underhand about it!"

Donald snorted. "If you wanted to know about your father, then you should've married me the thousand times I proposed it to you. You see, I planned to tell you about him as a wedding gift."

Angel's despair turned to horror. "You knew where he was?"

"I know everything, Angel. I knew he'd been released, almost a year ago. I thought about telling you, but I chose to say nothing, because the timing wasn't right. You would've abandoned me, and I couldn't have allowed that. That was why I intended to inform you about it, after we were married." He chuckled darkly. "Now, you will marry me, or I'll do to your father what I've done to that interfering constable."

"No..." She shook her head wretchedly. "Jimmy can't be dead. He can't be. He wasn't when I saw him last."

"I took care of it," Donald replied. "And, I'll repeat it as it seems as though you didn't quite hear me, I'll do the same thing to your father if you continue to resist my proposals. Although, I could just wait, and time would do the same thing."

Angel stared at him in disgust and confusion. "What do you mean?"

"Your father is very sick, Angel. He doesn't have much longer to live, so I suggest you make your decision quickly. Marry me, and I'll take you to see him, so you can say your farewells. Refuse me, and I'll keep you here until he's dead, so you'll know you missed the only opportunity you'll ever have to see him again."

He paused, menace rife in the air. "And I will claim you for myself anyway, regardless of your answer. I don't want to have to force myself upon you, but I will, if that's my only choice."

Tears streamed down her face as her mind descended into turmoil, and her heart shattered into a million pieces, like the brandy glass which had crashed to the ground the previous evening.

She had no reason to disbelieve Donald's words, for she had seen what his hired hand had done to Jimmy. It served Donald, to see the murderous job completed.

He's dead... He's dead, because of me. It took the last scrap of fight she had left in her, not to give up right there and then.

She would have done, had it not been for the fragile hope of seeing her father again. She could do nothing more for Jimmy, and that stung her to her core, but she could, at least, make peace with her father. She had to focus on that, or risk sinking into a pit of devastation from which she would never emerge. In such dire circumstances, what else could she do?

"You'll take me to my father, if I relent?" she said quietly, hating the words.

Donald grinned. "I will make the preparations, the moment you agree."

"Then… you've backed me into a corner, haven't you?"

"I should say I have." He cackled, his pugnacious features all the more foul in the anaemic glow of his lantern.

"Fine." It was the only thing she could bring herself to say, but Donald did not seem satisfied.

"Fine? What does that mean? I must have a clear answer, Angel."

She sighed, her throat raw from crying.

"I'll marry you. You've won. I'll marry you, as long as I get to see my father first."

In truth, she had no intention of actually marrying this vile specimen of a man. She merely needed to see her father, and then she would come up with another plan of action, once she had done so.

It would purchase her some much-needed time, to think of a means of escape.

She only hoped that an epiphany would come, before it was too late.

"A commendable decision." Donald stepped back towards the door. "I will make the preparations and then I will come for you, so we may go to him together. I'd rather like to see his face when I ask for your hand in marriage, not that his refusal would make the slightest bit of difference. The word of a dead man walking does not matter much."

With that, he opened the door and stepped out, before slamming it shut again and sliding the bolt closed.

In the ensuing, dark loneliness, Angel's mind turned back towards Jimmy. She thought of his face, bruised and swollen, and let fresh tears come.

She thought of their pleasant walk in the park, before it had soured, and wished she could reverse time, so she could urge him to run whilst he still had the chance.

But she could not change the past, any more than she could change the present. He was dead. She had cared for him, more than she dared to admit, and he had died because of it. He did not deserve this. And it was all her fault.

I will never forgive myself, not if I live a hundred years. She covered her face with her hands. *Forgive me, Jimmy. Please… forgive me.*

Chapter Twelve

Seconds and minutes felt like miniature lifetimes, as Angel waited for Donald to return. She had wept so much that her eyes itched, and her heart weighed heavy in its bone prison, thinking of the potential for love that she had destroyed, simply by being who she was.

Since her father had been taken away on that winter night, ten years ago, she had wondered if she had been born under an unlucky star, as the old wives' tale went.

Now, she felt certain that she had.

Yes, she would see her father again, if Donald stayed true to his word, but at such a hefty cost.

A man had died, a man she cared for, and she would lose her own life, in essence, for the chance to say goodbye to her beloved Papa.

I will lose him, too. So much time has been wasted... a year he's been free, and I didn't even know. She might have spent all of that year at his side, taking care of him and keeping him in comfort, had Donald spoken sooner.

He had robbed her of that, and he had robbed her of Jimmy, and she would have her revenge upon him, one way or another. He might have thought he was getting what he wanted, in marrying her, but she vowed, then and there, that she would pay him back in cruel kind. Yes, he would do well to sleep with one eye open.

Her head shot up as a loud bang ricocheted through the ship, followed by the thunderous beat of footsteps.

Screams pierced the air a moment later, prompting her to panic.

What was happening? Were the children all right? Had Donald done something?

She did not know, and the cacophony of sudden sounds were too confusing to make any sense of.

Jumping up, she ran for the door and beat her fists against it.

"Hello! Hello! Can anyone hear me?" she yelled, desperate to help the dear children.

A set of footsteps stopped abruptly. She heard the sound of the bolt being drawn back, before the door swept open to reveal the one man she had never expected to see.

"Jimmy!" she gasped, throwing herself into his arms.

"Easy there." He managed a pained laugh as he pushed her gently away. "I'm feeling a little… tender."

She blinked up at him and lifted a hand to touch his injured face. The swelling had worsened, shutting one of his eyes completely, whilst his lip was crusted with the remnants of blood, which had pooled from the wide split in his skin.

Every inch of his features was covered in the dappled bloom of bruising, but it was still him. Alive and mostly well, when she had thought him lost.

"I… thought you were dead." She stared deep into his one good eye.

He shook his head. "Almost, but not quite."

"But, how can you be here? How did you know where to find me?" It did not make sense.

"Your charming little friend, Sally, came to me at the hospital. She told me you were in trouble, so I rallied some men and I came to rescue you."

He took her hand in his, and kissed it gently, even with his injured lip.

"Although, I should warn you, she's a bit worried you might be cross with her. She says you told her to go to safety, but she disobeyed, because she wanted to make sure you were safe."

Angel's knees almost gave way beneath her. "Sally did this?"

"She did," he confirmed, with a pained smile. "She's as fond of you, as if you were her sister, or her mother."

"I'm no mother." She dropped her chin to her chest. "You have to understand, Jimmy. I'm not who you think I am. I do what I can for these children, but I've no choice but to send them out into the streets to steal. I used to be like them—I still am, sometimes.

But don't punish them for it, I beg of you! If you have to punish someone, then make it me."

Jimmy kissed her hand again. "The only person who is going to be punished is Donald McIntyre. The children will go free."

He gazed back at her.

"As for who you are, and what you are, I already know. And, though we probably shouldn't speak about it here, with so many constables present, I don't care. People are capable of change, if given the right opportunities. And people are dragged into lives they didn't ask for, if dealt a bad hand."

He reached out and pushed a strand of hair behind her ear.

"I know you didn't choose this life. Your father told me what happened, the night you were separated, and I put the rest together. You were a child, manipulated by an evil man. But you don't have to worry about that anymore. Donald will get what's coming to him, and he'll have attempted murder added to his sentence."

"My father..." She remembered what Jimmy had been about to say, before he had faded into unconsciousness in the park. "You know him? You've met him?"

He nodded. "I have."

"Is it true that he's... not well?"

Jimmy frowned. "Ah... that would explain it."

"Explain what?" she pressed.

"He tasked me with finding you, and said I had to be swift about it, though he didn't give me the reason. I suppose it'd make sense, if he's unwell." He interlaced his fingers with hers. "Come, let's go to him now, in case you're right. My men will take care of the children. I've already instructed them to bring every last child to the orphanage in Limehouse. It's a good one, run by a friend of mine. They'll be safe there."

Angel hesitated. "Do you promise?"

"I wouldn't lie to you." He smiled and gave her hand a squeeze.

"Then, let's go. Donald is a perpetual liar, but sometimes the truth he speaks can be far worse."

And she did not want to risk doubting him, if her father's life was truly on the line.

***

They arrived, by constabulary cart, a while later, outside the house on Chandler's Row. Jimmy, though hurt, helped her down and, together, they headed inside to find George Gilmour.

After speaking with the landlady, they were directed up to the top of the house, to the attic apartment where George resided. The door was open, allowing them easy entry.

Angel looked around in dismay, for the apartments were nothing short of squalid, with tattered curtains and a filthy floor that did not look as though it had been cleaned in a long while.

However, she did not linger for long, as she headed for a door at the back of the main space.

Turning the handle, she pushed it open to find her father lying upon a narrow bed, curled up in a foetal position as the sunlight glanced in through the window, touching his face like a kindly nurse.

"Papa?" she whispered, fearing she had come too late.

Her father stirred, his body twisting as he lifted his head to see who spoke. His eyes flew wide as he saw her, standing there. "Angel? Is it really you? Am I dreaming?"

She rushed to his side and clutched for his hand. "No, Papa, you're not dreaming. I'm here. Constable Milton found me, and he brought me to you." She knew that, in this instance, Donald had not been lying.

Her father looked very ill, indeed. Bones protruded through his papery skin, and his body possessed a skeletal quality that alarmed her.

His eyes were ringed with dark crescents, and his lips were dry and cracked, and drained of all colour.

Nevertheless, her father smiled. "He found you? I knew I could rely on him."

"I'm sorry it's taken me so long, Papa. I didn't know you'd been released. I didn't even know you were still alive." She leant over and pressed her forehead against his chest as more tears came.

In all her life, she could not remember crying so much.

"Hush now, sweetheart," he urged. "You weren't to know. I tried to find you, but no-one knew where you were. I followed every trail until it ran cold, but it was as if you'd vanished. I thought I was being punished for my past deeds. I thought I was being punished for abandoning you, that night. I thought I'd die without ever seeing you again."

"You're not going to die," she murmured, half-pleading.

He raised his hand to her hair and stroked it softly. "I am, little one. I've known it for some time. But you're here, and I've been allowed this last gift of seeing you again, and... now, I'm not so afraid."

He put his arms around her and held her close.

"And, though I couldn't take care of you these past ten years, I've made sure that you'll have security when I finally pass from this world. I've worked hard, Angel, and I've worked honestly. Everything I've earned, and everything I have, will belong to you when I die."

She shook her head, burying her face deeper into his chest. "I don't want what you've earned. I want you to stay. I don't want you to die, Papa. Please, don't go."

"Don't make me hate God for taking me away from you, Angel." He held her tighter. "I can't stay, but I can go with dignity and peace. I can go, knowing I've seen you, and that you're going to be taken care of. But, there's one thing I must ask of you."

"Anything," she sobbed.

"Do you forgive me?" he whispered. "I didn't mean to leave you alone that night. I thought they'd let me go, and I'd be able to come back, just as I promised. I'm sorry that I didn't. I'm sorry that I left you. I'm sorry for the life you've had to live, because of it."

A guttural cry escaped her throat. "Forgive you? There's nothing to forgive. I've missed you, every day of these last ten years. I've wanted nothing more than to see you again, in case you thought I blamed you. I don't. I wouldn't. I love you, Papa."

He smiled against her shoulder. "Then I can die a happy man. A loved man. And know this—I love you, my sweet Angel. You helped me survive ten years. You are dearer to me than my own life. But you have to promise me that you'll live well, and you'll find happiness in this world? Please, Angel. Promise me that."

"I'll try, Papa."

She clung onto him with everything she had, until the gut-wrenching moment she realised that he was no longer holding onto her.

Slowly, she pulled away, to find him lying motionless, his eyes staring vacantly out towards the window.

A smile graced his lips, as though some divine entity had entered through that windowpane and collected him, to take him to a better place. Her dear father had died, having held on just long enough to see her again.

"I'm sorry, Angel." Jimmy appeared at her side, his eyes glittering with tears.

"He's gone, Jimmy… he's gone." She could hardly believe it, her heart sinking like a stone.

He edged closer. "I know, Angel. I'm so very sorry."

With one hand gripping her father's, she turned and buried herself in Jimmy's embrace, as his arms wrapped around her. And he held onto her far tighter than any person had ever held her before.

Here, in his arms, she felt truly safe, for Jimmy had brought her to her father's side, just in time to say goodbye. And she knew that, no matter how long she lived, she would never be able to repay that debt of gratitude. However, perhaps, she could love him... and, perhaps, that would be close enough.

Epilogue

"And how are the wayward urchins today, my love?" Jimmy rapped on the open door of the school room and beamed at his wife.

Angel chuckled, listening to the sound of the children's laughter outside the window. "As mischievous as ever, but they are learning, and that's all I can ask of them."

Jimmy came into the room and walked through the desks towards her, and she rose from her chair to meet him.

He lifted a hand to her cheek and bent his head, catching her lips in hers as he planted a delicious kiss there. Her hands went to his waist, holding onto him as she kissed him back, sinking into the romantic familiarity as her stomach fluttered with butterflies.

Even after three years of marriage, he never failed to make her heart race. With him, she had found everything she had ever wanted, though it had taken her some time to realise that love could be possible.

"I hope they're not being too rambunctious." He smoothed a hand across her rounded belly, where their own child grew within her. "You've got this little one to think of, and I won't have anyone working you too hard."

She smiled with pure elation. "I've enough love and patience for all of them… and some left for you."

"Then I'm fortunate indeed, to have but a scrap of your love." He laughed, and kissed her again, with slow passion.

"Come, you know you've got the lion's share." She looped her arms about his neck and lay her head on his shoulder, as they swayed gently to silent music.

Much had changed in the three years since Donald's arrest and her father's death. With the money her father had left her, she had trained to be a schoolmistress, before taking up a position at the very orphanage in Limehouse where Jimmy had placed all of the children from the pickpocketing gang.

Some of the orphans had not settled well into a more docile, legal life, and she was sorry for that, but the majority had flourished. Now, she got to watch them, and other unfortunate children, take to their studies and garner themselves an education that would see them towards a better life.

Indeed, there had already been a number of successes. Leon had become a fully-fledged apprentice to Mr. Phelps, the merchant, and often visited Angel.

Meanwhile, Sally had become something of a daughter to her, living with her and Jimmy in their pleasant apartments on the outskirts of Poplar.

And Angel went to the cemetery where Solomon and her father were buried, almost every week, to make sure that neither of them ever felt abandoned.

As for Donald McIntyre, he had been given his comeuppance. As it turned out, it did not serve a person well to make an attempt on the life of a constable. As well as being charged with theft, he had been given the death sentence for trying to kill Jimmy. None had mourned him, and Angel liked to think that London was a safer place without him in it, though she did not like the idea of anyone being killed, for any reason.

"I love you, Angel." Jimmy pulled back slightly and gazed into her eyes.

She smiled up at him. "Not nearly as much as I love you."

"Now, you know that's not true."

She knew better than to protest aloud, for he always won, but in the privacy of her thoughts, she contested his words. *No, Jimmy, it is true. I love you more than I thought it possible to love anyone. And I will always love you more than you love me, because you gave me my father back, however temporarily, and there is nothing in this world that could beat that.*

Thanks to him, she had reconciled her past with her present, and she could look forward to a future of blissful happiness, all because he had stopped to speak with her that day, when Solomon had died. And he had proven, beyond all doubt, that no matter who you were, or what you did, it did not define a person. Everyone was capable of change, and he had changed her world irrevocably, in the most remarkable way.

THE END

Would you like a FREE Book?

Join Iris Coles Newsletter

HERE

Printed in Great Britain
by Amazon